The Battle Lost and Won

ALSO BY OLIVIA MANNING

The Wind Changes
The Remarkable Expedition
Growing Up (short stories)
Artist Among the Missing
School for Love
A Different Face
The Doves of Venus
My Husband Cartwright (short stories)

The Balkan Trilogy

The Great Fortune
The Spoilt City
Friends and Heroes

A Romantic Hero (short stories)
The Play Room
The Rain Forest

The Levant Trilogy

The Danger Tree

The Battle Lost and Won

A NOVEL BY

OLIVIA MANNING

WEIDENFELD AND NICOLSON
LONDON

First published in Great Britain by
Weidenfeld and Nicolson
91 Clapham High Street   London SW4

ISBN 0 297 77540 5

Printed and bound in Great Britain by
Morrison & Gibb Ltd, London and Edinburgh

TO PARVIN AND MICHAEL LAURENCE

THE BATTLE LOST AND WON *is the second of three novels set in Egypt, the first of which was* THE DANGER TREE, *and continues the story of some of the characters from 'The Balkan Trilogy'.*

THE BATTLE LOST AND WON *begins just before Alamein.*

1

Simon Boulderstone, coming into Cairo on leave, passed the pyramids at Giza when they were hazed over by mid-day heat. The first time he had seen them, he had been struck with wonder, but now there was no wonder left in the world. His brother, Hugo, had been killed. That very morning, in the dark, early hours, Hugo had bled to death in no-man's-land.

Simon had stopped a lorry on the coast road east of Alamein and, alone in the back, had cried himself to sleep. Now that he would have to face the two men in front, he tried to wipe away the marks of tears but did not do it very well. The lorry stopped outside Mena House. The driver, coming round to speak to Simon, stared at him then said, 'You've caught the sun, sir,' as though they had not, all of them, been broiled by sun during the long summer months.

'You want anywhere in particular, sir?'

'A cheap hotel, if you know of one.'

The driver suggested the International and Simon said, 'Glad if you'd drop me there.' They drove on through the suburbs into the centre of Cairo where the lorry stopped again. They were at a modern Midan, a meeting place of three small streets where the old houses were being pulled down and replaced by concrete blocks. One of the blocks was the International and it had the unadorned air of cheapness.

Throwing down his kit, Simon thanked the two men then jumped down himself. Standing on the pavement, in the dazzling light, he seemed to be in a trance, and the driver asked him: 'You all right, sir?'

Simon nodded and the lorry went on. Left alone in the middle of the Midan, he stared at a palm tree that rose from a bed of ashy sand. As he observed it, he began to feel an extraordinary poignancy about it so for a few minutes he could not move but, forgetting Hugo, he centred his misery on this solitary palm. From its height and the length of its fronds, he could guess it was an old tree that had grown in other, more spacious days. Now, seeing it hemmed in by buildings like a bird in too small a cage, he ached with pity for it though the tree itself conveyed no sense of deprivation. A human being in similar case would have been bemoaning his misfortune but the tree, swaying in the hot wind, spread itself as though rejoicing in such air and light as came to it.

Feeling near to weeping again, he said aloud, 'Am I going crazy or something?' and picked up his kit.

The hotel, its windows shuttered against the sun, looked empty but there was a clerk in the hall, staring in boredom at the glass entrance doors. The sight of Simon brought him to life: 'Yes, please? You wan' room? You wan' bather?'

Simon, sun-parched, sweat-soaked, unshaven, sand in hair and eyes, needed a bath though he was too deep in grief to feel the want of anything. He was taken upstairs to a small room with a bathroom so narrow, the bath fitted into it like a foot into a shoe. Filling the bath, he lay comatose in luke-warm water until he heard the hotel waking up.

He could see through his bedroom window that the dusty saffron colour of the afternoon had deepened into the ochre of early evening. Time had extended itself in his desolation, yet it was still the day on which Hugo had died. At this pace, how was he to endure the rest of his life? How, as a mere beginning, was he to get through the week ahead?

He looked at himself in his shaving mirror, expecting to see himself ravaged by his emotion but the face that looked back at him was still a very young face, burnt by the sun, a little dried by the desert wind, but untouched by the sorrow of that day.

He was twenty years of age. Hugo had been his senior by a year and they were as alike as twins. Imagining Hugo's body disintegrating in the sand, he felt a spasm of raging indignation against this early death, and then he thought of those who must suffer with him: his parents, his relatives and the girl Edwina whom he thought of as Hugo's girl. He had seen Edwina when he first came to Cairo and he realised, with a slight lift of spirit, that he now had good reason to see her again.

Having somewhere to go, something to do, he shaved and dressed carefully and went out to streets that were stale with the hot and dusty end of summer.

The office workers were returning to work after the siesta. They crowded the tram-cars, hanging in bunches at every entrance, while the superior officials had taken all the taxis. Simon managed to find an empty gharry but this made so little progress among the traffic that he could have walked more quickly.

Heat hung like a fog in the air, a coppery fog coloured by the light of the sinking sun. As they came down to the embankment, the river, slowly turning and lifting the feluccas towards the sea, was a fiery gold. On the western side, the pyramids had come into view, triangles of black no bigger than a thumb-nail.

In among the ramshackle houses of Garden City, Simon breathed the evening smell of jasmin and, in spite of himself, felt the excitement of being there. Before he left England, he had received a letter from Hugo telling him to buy scent for Edwina at a West End shop. The scent was to travel in the diplomatic bag and Simon, overawed, had taken it to the Foreign Office where the young man who accepted it said, 'Another votive offering for Miss Little?' The scent was called *Gardenia* but gardenias and jasmin were all one to Simon and the whole of Garden City was for him permeated by the delicious sweetness of Edwina Little.

When the gharry reached his destination, he looked up at the balcony of the upper flat, half-expecting to find Edwina still standing there as she had stood that day, his second day in Egypt. He thought, 'Poor Edwina, poor girl!' and there was a sort of morose comfort in the fact she too would suffer their loss.

Several people lived in the flat. One of them, a young woman called Harriet Pringle, was in the living-room when he entered it.

She started up, saying, 'Hugo?' but knowing it could not be Hugo.

'No, it's Simon . . .' Simon's voice broke and Harriet, giving him time to control himself, said: 'Yes, of course it's Simon. Do you remember me? We climbed the Great Pyramid together.'

He still could not speak and Harriet, sensing the reason for his grief, took his arm and led him to a chair. He sat down, blinking to keep back his tears that came in a slow, painful trickle, nothing like the fierce bout of weeping that had overwhelmed him in the back of the lorry. He scrubbed his handkerchief over his cheeks and apologised for his weakness.

'I've come to see Edwina and tell her . . . Hugo has been killed.'

Hassan, the safragi, looking for drama, was peering round the door. Harriet, who had taken over the housekeeping, told him to bring in the drinks trolley. Wheeling it in, he observed Simon with furtive curiosity and Harriet ordered him away.

She gave Simon a half-glass of whisky and as he sipped it, he spoke more easily: 'He was out with a patrol, picking up the wounded. They were all killed. Hugo's legs were blown off and he bled to death. His batman found him and sat beside him till he died. There was a sandstorm, so it wasn't possible to get him back. Too late, anyway. He just lay there and bled to death.'

'I'm sorry.' Harriet was deeply sorry but not shocked. When she said goodbye to Hugo, on his last leave, a voice in her head had said, 'He won't come back. He is going to die.'

'I have to tell Edwina. It's terrible for her.'

'And for everyone who knew him.'

'But she was special. I mean: she was Hugo's girl.'

Harriet made no reply but remained silent for a while then, standing up, said, 'I'll go and find her.' As she went through the baize door that led to the bedroom corridor, Edwina was coming out of the bathroom with a white bath-robe round her shoulders. She worked at the British Embassy but that day she had stayed at home with a hang-over that she called a migraine.

'Are you better?'

'Oh, much better.' Edwina smiled at Harriet, an amused,

conniving smile because, however bad her headache, she was always well enough to go out in the evening. As she hurried into her room, she said, 'Come and talk to me while I dress. Peter will be here any minute.'

She stood naked, tall and shapely, her skin glistening from the bath, and slapped herself dry with a swansdown puff. Harriet, watching her as she prepared for her night with Peter Lisdoon-varna, said, 'Edwina' with a warning emphasis that brought Edwina to a stop. She stared at Harriet, puzzled.

'What is it, Harriet?'

'Simon Boulderstone is here.'

'You mean Hugo, don't you?'

'No, it's the younger one: Simon. Edwina, he's brought bad news. Hugo has been killed.'

'Oh, no. Not Hugo? What a pity! I *am* sorry.' Edwina stood, reflectively still a moment, then, shaking her head regretfully, went to her chest of drawers and putting her hand in among her satin, crêpe-de-Chine and lace underclothes, said again, 'I am sorry,' but her mind was on other things. She had been fond of Hugo but she could not mourn him just then.

'Edwina, listen! Simon's under the impression that you were Hugo's girl. He expects you to be terribly upset.'

'But of course I'm upset. Hugo was one of the nicest boys I knew – gentle, sweet, generous. We got on well and we had a wonderful time when he came on leave. I was really fond of him.'

'Simon thinks you were in love. Don't disillusion him. Don't . . .' Harriet was going to say 'Don't hurt him' but said instead: 'Don't disappoint him.'

Edwina sighed and put a slip over her head then, crossing to Harriet, she took Harriet's hands into her own and said in a small, persuasive voice: 'Darling, I can't see him now with Peter coming any minute. Be a dear. Tell him I'm at the office. Ask him to come back tomorrow.'

'He knows you're here.'

Edwina sighed again: 'What *can* I do?' She dropped Harriet's hands and went to the wardrobe and took out a draped, white evening gown. Hanging it on the door in readiness, she looked in the glass: 'M'face – how awful!'

She touched in her eyes and lips, stepped into the dress, then returning to the chest of drawers, chose one of a long row of large, ornamental scent bottles and said, 'I think he gave me this.' She caught her breath and held her head back, trying to contain her tears. Dabbing the scent on her skin, enhancing the gardenia scent of the room, she murmured, 'These poor boys! You meet them . . . you . . .' She paused, catching her breath.

'You give them your heart?'

'Yes. And then they go back and get killed.' Edwina, putting her forefingers under her lashes to lift the wetness away, said, 'Oh, dear!' and, sniffing, gave Harriet a rueful smile that was a comment both on the futility of grief and her own incorrigible frivolity: 'What's to be done about it? Cry one's self sick? What good would that do?'

She might have given herself up to weeping were she not expecting Peter. Instead, she said anxiously, 'Can't let him see me like this,' and began to mend her make-up.

Harriet, feeling her anxiety, thought how precarious must be her hold on Peter Lisdoonvarna if she dared not betray pity for a young man's death. And it was not that Peter was prone to jealousy. She knew that any hint of affection for another man would be used by him as excuse for his own philanderings.

'How do I look?'

A current of air, bringing into the scented room the fresh smell of the tamarisks, stirred the white dress that hung like a peplos from Edwina's wide, brown shoulders.

'You look like the statue of Athena.'

'Oh, Harriet!' Edwina, a beauty but not a classical beauty, laughed at this praise. Then, hearing Peter's footsteps in the corridor, turned in expectation, putting her hands together. He was a broad, heavy man and the dry wooden floor cracked under his weight. Throwing open the door without knocking, he asked loudly: 'What's going on out there? Chap blubbing in the living-room!'

Harriet said, 'His brother's just been killed.'

14

'Oh, I say!' Peter, contrite, lowered his voice: 'Tough luck!' His big face with its saddle nose and black moustache, expressed as much concern as any soldier could feel after three years of desert warfare: 'Poor blighter's taking it hard, eh? Should have said a few words of sympathy.'

Peter's tone made evident his belief that his sympathy would give more than usual comfort to an inferior for he was, as everyone knew or pretended not to know, an Irish peer. Titles were out for the duration, to the annoyance of Levantine hostesses who greatly loved them, and Peter called himself Colonel Lisdoonvarna.

Now, having given a thought to Simon's condition, he looked up cheerfully: 'You ready, old girl? I've booked at the Continental roof garden. You like that?'

'You know I do.'

Peter led the two women back to the living-room where Simon disconsolately sat alone. At the sight of Edwina, he jumped up, looking at her with admiration that, for the moment, transcended grief.

Crossing to him, Edwina said quietly: 'Oh, Simon, I'm so sorry,' and Simon, longing to touch her, raised his hands. He seemed about to hold her in an embrace of commiseration but Peter, stepping forward and putting her on one side, took over the situation, dominating it as a right.

He spoke briskly to Simon: 'Sorry to hear what happened, old chap. I know how you feel. Knocks you sideways for a time, but we all have to face up to these things. Fortunes of war, y'know. You in for a spot of leave?'

'I've got seven days.'

'Good for you. Splendid. I've a table booked for supper so we have to be on our way, but see you again, I hope.'

Swinging round, Peter put a possessive hand on Edwina's shoulder and said, 'Come along, old girl.'

Simon, realising Peter's ascendancy over her, turned on Edwina with a dazed and questioning expression that disturbed her. She said, 'I've forgotten my handkerchief,' and ran back to her room.

Peter returned his attention to Simon: 'Envy you, y'know.

Long to be back at the front m'self. Can't stand the "Armchair" set-up.'

Simon stared at him for a moment then did his best to respond: 'You wouldn't want to be where I am, sir.' He explained that his unit was a 'Jock' column that patrolled the southern sector of the line: 'The fighting's always somewhere else.'

'Still, you're not in a damned silly office. You're leading a man's life.'

Simon agreed. He said the life suited him. If the patrols were uneventful he was compensated by the comradeship of the men.

Harriet, watching them as they talked, saw Peter avoiding a direct glance at Simon whose eyes were still red, while Simon was regaining his vitality. The worst, the most immediate, pain of loss was over and, soon enough, Hugo, for all of them, would be no more than a sad memory at the back of the mind.

Simon was saying there was one thing he enjoyed in the desert. He enjoyed finding his way around. 'I've got a sense of the place, somehow. I feel I belong there.' That morning, in despair, he would have been glad never to see the desert again. Now, envied and infected by Peter's approval of desert life, he said, 'To tell you the truth, I'll be glad to get back there. I'd like to have a real go at the bastards. They killed my brother when he was with an ambulance, bringing in the wounded. They shot them up. They knew what they were doing. I feel I owe them one.'

'That's the spirit.' Peter took a diary from an inner pocket: 'If you'd like a transfer, I might work it. A chap who's good at finding his way round has his uses in the desert. You could become a liaison officer. Would that appeal to you?'

Simon, feeling guilty that this day of misfortune might also be the day of opportunity, blushed and said, 'It would indeed, sir.'

Edwina, returning to the room as Peter was noting down Simon's name and position at the front, was relieved to find the men on easy terms. She gave Simon a conciliatory smile then, watching Peter as he wrote, stood, waiting, with a sort of avid patience until he was ready for her.

Putting the diary back in his pocket, he said, 'Right, I'll start things moving,' then he called to Edwina: 'Come along,' and she followed him obediently from the flat.

Simon, looking after them, at once forgot the proposed transfer, and felt only amazement that Edwina, who had been Hugo's girl, should now be subject to this heavy-featured colonel. It had seemed to him that while Edwina shared his love for Hugo, Hugo was not completely dead. Remembering Hugo's looks, his gentleness, his absolute niceness, he felt these qualities slighted – and yet, what good would they be to her now?

Harriet, pitying his downcast face, said: 'You'll stay to supper, won't you?'

'No. No thank you.' Simon felt he only wanted to get away from this room which held Edwina's lingering fragrance, but did not know where he would go. This flat, because it was Edwina's flat, had had for him a glowing, beckoning quality, and he knew nowhere else in Cairo. He did not know the name of any street except the one in the army song: the Berka. That was where the men went to find bints.

'Well, have another drink before you go.'

Realising he had no heart for bints that evening, Simon let Harriet refill his glass and asked: 'Who is this Colonel Lisdoon-varna? It's an unusual name.'

'It's an Irish name. He's Lord Lisdoonvarna but, as you know, we don't use titles these days.'

'I see.' Simon did indeed see. The fact that Peter was a peer solved a mystery but the solution was more painful than his earlier perplexity. He sat silent, glass in hand, not drinking, hearing the safragi laying the supper table. If he were going, he should go now, but instead he sat on, too dispirited to move.

The front door opened and another occupant of the flat entered the room. This was a woman older than Edwina or Harriet, delicately built with dark eyes and a fine, regular face.

Coming in quickly, saying 'Hello' to Harriet, she gave an impression of genial gaiety, an impression that surprised Simon who had recognised her at once. She was Lady Hooper. He had been one of a picnic party that had gone uninvited to the Hoopers' house in the Fayoum and had blundered in on tragedy.

17

Harriet said, 'Angela, do you remember Simon Boulderstone?'

'Yes, I remember.' Whether the memory was painful or not, she smiled happily on Simon and taking his hand, held it as she said: 'You were the young officer who was in the room when I brought in my little boy. We didn't know he was dead, you know: or perhaps we couldn't bear to know. It must have been upsetting for you. I'm sorry.' Angela gazed at Simon, still smiling and waited as though there was point in apologising so long after the event.

Harriet said, 'I'm afraid Simon has another reason to be upset. His brother has been killed.'

'Oh, poor boy!' She placed her other hand on top of his and held on to him: 'So we are both bereaved! You will stay with us, won't you?' She turned to Harriet to ask: 'Who's in tonight? What about Guy?' Guy was Harriet's husband. Harriet shook her head. 'Not Guy, that goes without saying. And Edwina's out with Peter. It's Dobson's night on duty at the Embassy, so that leaves only us and Percy Gibbon.'

'Percy Gibbon! Oh lord, that's good reason to go out. Let's take this beautiful young man into the world. Let's flaunt him.' She laughed at Simon and squeezed his hand: 'Where would you like to go?'

'I don't know. I've never been anywhere in Cairo. I haven't even been to the Berka.'

'Oh, oh, oh!' Angela's amusement was such that she dropped back on to the sofa taking Simon with her: 'You dreadful creature, wanting to visit the Berka!'

Simon reddened in his confusion: 'I didn't mean I wanted . . . It's just that the men talk about it. It's the only street name I know.'

This renewed Angela's laughter and Simon, watching her as she wiped her eyes and said 'Oh dear, oh dear!', was disturbed by this gaiety and wondered how she could so quickly put death out of mind. Yet he smiled and Harriet, also disturbed by Angela's light-hearted behaviour, was relieved to see his smile.

'Let's send Hassan out for a taxi.' Angela turned to Harriet: 'If we're going on the tiles, we'll need more male protection.

Where shall we find it? How about the Union? Who's likely to be there?'

'Castlebar, I imagine.'

Angela who had left her husband after her son's death, had come to live in Dobson's flat hoping, as she said, to find congenial company. She had found Harriet and through her had met Castlebar. The mention of Castlebar was a joke between them and Harriet explained to Simon.

'Castlebar haunts the place. When he's not sitting on the lawn, it's as though a familiar tree had been cut down.'

Listening to this, Angela became restless and broke in to say: 'Come on. Let's get going.'

Hassan, told to find them a taxi, goggled in indignation: 'No need taxi. All food on table now.' Forced out on what he saw as a superfluous task, he came back with a gharry and said, 'No taxis, not anywhere.'

Angela, taking it for granted that Simon would accompany them, led him down to the gharry and sat beside him. As the gharry ambled through Garden City to the main road, she held him tightly by the hand and talked boisterously so, whether he wanted to come or not, he was given no chance to refuse.

Bemused by all that was happening, he thought of her carrying the dead child into the Fayoum house, and felt she was beyond his understanding. He tried to ease his hand away but she would not let him go and so, still clasped like lovers, they crossed the dark water towards the riverside lights of Gezira.

There was no moon. The lawns of the Anglo-Egyptian Union were lit by the windows of the club house and the bright, greenish light of the Officers' Club that faced it. At the edge of the lawn, old trees, that had grown to a great height, crowded their heads darkly above the tables set out for the club members.

Having conducted Simon into the club, Angela let him go and walked on ahead, apparently looking for someone who was not there. When they sat down at a table, she was subdued as though disappointed.

Unlike the other members who were drinking coffee or Stella beer, Angela ordered a bottle of whisky and told the safragi to bring half a dozen glasses. Her advent at the Union a few weeks before had caused a sensation, but she was a sensation no longer. The Union membership comprised university lecturers, teachers of English and others of the poorer English sort while Angela was known to be a rich woman who mixed with the Cairo gambling, polo-playing set. Her nightly order of a bottle of whisky had startled the safragis at first but now it was brought without question.

Harriet, who did not like whisky, was given wine but Simon accepted the glass poured for him though he did not drink it. When they were all served, the bottle was placed like a beacon in the middle of the table and almost at once it drew Castlebar from the snooker table.

Harriet, from where she sat, could see his figure wavering through the shadows, drooping and edging round the table, coming with cautious purpose towards the bottle, like an animal that keeps to windward of its prey. He paused a couple of yards from the table and Angela, knowing he was there, smiled to herself.

Though their friendship seemed to have sprung up fully grown, he edged forward with sly diffidence, still unable to believe in his good fortune. And, Harriet thought, he might well be diffident for it was beyond her to understand what Angela saw in him.

Harriet was not the only one critical of this middle-aged teacher-poet who had the broken-down air of a man to whom money spent on anything but drink and cigarettes was money wasted. As they observed his circuitous approach, people murmured together, their faces keen with curiosity and dis-approval. When he made the last few feet towards her, Angela jerked her head round and laughed as though he had pulled off a clever trick.

'H-h-hello, there!' he stammered, trying to sound hearty.

'Welcome. Sit beside me. Have a drink.'

Doing as he was bid, Castlebar made a deprecating noise, mumbling: 'Must let me put something in the kitty.'

'No. My treat.'

Castlebar did not argue. Taking whisky into his mouth, he held it there, moving it round his gums in ruminative appreciation, then let it slide slowly down his throat. After this, he went through his usual ritual of placing a cigarette packet squarely in front of him, one cigarette propped ready to hand so there need be no interval between smokes. As he concentrated on getting the cigarette upright, Angela smiled indulgently. All set, he raised his thick, pale eyelids and they exchanged a long, meaningful look.

Angela whispered, 'Any news?'

'I had a cable. She says she'll get back by hook or by crook.'

They were talking of Castlebar's wife who had gone on holiday to England and been marooned there by the outbreak of war. The threat of her return hung over Angela who said, 'But surely she won't make it?'

Castlebar giggled: 'S⁄s⁄she's a p⁄p⁄pretty ruthless bitch. If anyone can do it, she will.' He appeared to take pride in having such a wife and Angela, raising her brows, turned from him until he made amends.

'Don't worry. She'll tread on anyone's face to get what she wants, but it won't work this time. Why should they send her out?' Castlebar slid his hand across the table towards her and she bent and gave it a rapid kiss.

Their enclosed intimacy embarrassed Simon, who looked away, while Harriet, feeling excluded, was envious and depressed. Guy could be affectionate but he never lost consciousness of the outside world. It was always there for him and its claim on him had caused dissension between them.

Leaving Angela and Castlebar to their communion, she asked Simon about his army life. When they had climbed the pyramid together, they had sat at the top and talked of the war in the desert. He had said, 'I don't know what it's like out there,' but now he knew and she asked him how he spent his days.

'Not doing much. We're so far from the main positions, there seems no point in being there.'

'But of course there is a point?'

'Oh yes. I asked our sergeant once. I said, "What's the use, our being here, bored stiff and doing nothing?" and he said, "What'd happen if we weren't here?" You can see what he meant.'

A taxi came in the gate and a man, jumping down and hurriedly settling with the driver, came to the whisky as though it had sent a call out to him. This new arrival was Castlebar's friend, Jake Jackman, who described himself as a freelance journalist, but what he really did, not even Castlebar could say. His aquiline face, though not unhandsome, was spoilt by an aggrieved expression that became more aggrieved when he saw Angela and Castlebar holding hands. Still, Angela was the owner of the bottle and he had to accept things as they were. Forced to show her some courtesy, he stretched his lips in a momentary smile and saying, 'Mind if I join you?' sat down before she could reply. She laughed and pushed the bottle towards him. Having taken a drink, he bent forward and pulling at his long beak of a nose, looked angrily at Simon: 'I suppose *you're* wondering why I'm not in uniform?'

Simon began to disclaim any such interest but Jackman was not listening. Having distracted Angela and Castlebar from each other, he told them: 'You know that old bag Rutter? Got too much money for her own good. Saw her at Groppi's this after-noon and what do you think she said? She said, "Young man why aren't you in uniform?" Impertinent old cow!'

Castlebar giggled: 'What did you say?'

'I said, "Madam, if you think I'll sacrifice my life to preserve you and your bank balance, you've got another think coming." That ruffled the old hen's feathers. She said, "You're a very rude young man!" "You're dead right, missus," I said.' Having recounted his story, Jackman sat up, willing to think of other things: 'You people going somewhere to eat?'

Angela looked tenderly at Castlebar: 'What do you want to do, Bill?'

Castlebar, lowering his eyelids, smiled, conveying his future plans, but for the moment he was content to eat: 'We might get a bite somewhere.'

'The Extase, then,' Angela said and Jackman jumped up, ready to depart.

They could have walked to the Extase, which was on the river bank at Bulaq, but Angela waved to a taxi at the gate and it took them across the bridge. The fare was only a few piastres and Angela allowed Castlebar to settle it while she went into the Extase to pay the entrance fees. Simon, unused to her largesse, hurried after her, offering his share, but she closed his hand over the notes he was holding and led him inside, a captive guest.

Harriet had her own ways of repaying Angela's hospitality and so, no doubt, had Castlebar, but Jackman accepted it without question, having once said to Harriet, 'If Angela insists on taking us to places we can't afford, then it's up to her. She knows I haven't the lolly for these parties.' This might be true but, Harriet noted, he was, more often than not, self-invited.

Inside the open-air night club, there was the usual crowd of officers and such girls as they could find. The officers, most of them on leave, were drunk or nearly drunk, and there was an atmosphere of uproar.

As they queued for a table, Harriet said to Angela: 'Aren't you suffocated by all this noise?'

Angela's laughter rose above it: 'Can't get enough of it.'

The Extase, being so close to the river, was held to be cooler than other places but the arc lights poured heat down on the guests and the guests, amorous and sweating, generated more heat. It was not a place Harriet much liked. On a previous visit she had seen Guy with Edwina, and the shock of this sight still remained with her although Guy had protested he was merely comforting Edwina, who was distressed because Peter had failed to keep a date. Looking towards the table where they had been seated, she felt an impulse to run from the place – but she had nowhere to go and no one to go with.

When their turn came to be led to a table, Angela gave an excited scream and pointed to the people at the next table. One of them was a friend and Angela demanded that the tables be placed together so the two parties could become one. She introduced the friend as, 'Mortimer'. Mortimer, a plain girl with a pleasant

23

expression and a sun reddened skin, was in uniform of a sort and had with her two young captains in the regiment that was nick-named 'the Cherrypickers'.

Looking round the double table, Angela said, 'Isn't this fun?' and Mortimer, mellow with drink, agreed, 'Great fun', but there was no response from the others.

Though the tables were united, there was division between the factions. The two hussars, called Terry and Tony, had been drinking champagne and were in an elated condition. They took no notice of Simon but the other men, Castlebar and Jackman, roused in them a hostile merriment. They stared unbelievingly at them then, turning to each other, fell together with gusts of laughter that brought tears to their eyes.

Mortimer chided them, 'Come on, now, boys!' but they were beyond her control.

To make matters worse, another non-combatant, one who had experienced Angela's liberality in the past, approached the party and stood there like a mendicant, begging to be allowed in. He was Major Cookson, who, having lost all his Greek property and knowing no life but a life of pleasure, hung around places like the Extase and provided lonely officers with telephone numbers. Harriet, meeting his humble, pleading gaze, felt discomfited but it was not for her to invite him to the table. Angela was too absorbed with her talk to notice him and so he stood, a very thin, epicene figure, much aged by his changed circumstances, the nubbled surface of his silk suit brushed with grime and his buckskin shoes, more grey than white, breaking at the sides.

Harriet thought 'The war has done for us all' though, in fact, she and Guy were more fortunate than many. Because they had known Dobson in Bucharest, they had been lifted out of the clutter of refugees and given a room in his Embassy flat. She looked down at her own sandals, whitened each morning by the servants, and felt pleased with them. Yet, how curious it was that they could raise her self-esteem!

Cookson's behaviour during the evacuation from Greece had given her no cause to respect him but now, seeing him there old, dry, brittle, seedy, like a piece of seaweed that circumstances had cast above the tide line, she was sorry for him. She touched Angela's arm and whispered to her. Angela, turning at once, called to him: 'Major Cookson, have you come to join us?'

A chair was found and Cookson was fitted in between Harriet and Castlebar. As he stretched a gaunt hand towards Castlebar's cigarette pack, Castlebar with a snarling glance, like one hungry dog espying another, moved it out of reach.

The Cherrypickers now found a new object for their scornful regard. As they stared at him, Cookson, probably attracted by their virile, youthful good looks, grew red and cast down his eyes. Terry, leaning towards him, enquired: 'Did Lady Hooper say *Major* Cookson?'

Cookson gave a brief, unhappy nod. His rank, acquired during the First War, was said by his enemies to have been acting and unpaid. Terry now asked with elaborate courtesy: 'Brigade of Guards, weren't you?' This time Cookson gave a brief, unhappy shake of the head.

Terry looked at Tony: 'There was a Cookson in the Guards, wasn't there? You must have known him?'

Tony heartily agreed: 'Jove, yes. Dear old Cookson. We used to call him Queenie. Had a queer way of sitting, Cookson had. Chaps used to ask "Why is Queenie like an engine?"'

Terry, knowing the answer to that one, put his hands over his eyes and howled with laughter.

Simon, too, knew the answer to that one and it increased his nervous disgust with the people about him. Because of his youth and silence, he was ignored by most of them but that did not worry him. What did worry him was their strangeness and hilarity. There were only eight of them but for all the sense he could make of the party, there might have been a couple of dozen. Even the Cherrypickers, on leave as he was, seemed to him unreal in their ribald insolence. He had never known men behave so badly in company. He was shocked. And, he remembered, it was still the day on which Hugo had died.

There was a pause while a small boy put glasses on the table, and a Nubian safragi, dripping sweat on to the customers, brought champagne in a bucket. Breaking the wire with his hand, he let the cork fly away. The ice had melted and the champagne, a gritty, sweetish German brand, was warm. Food came with the same lack of ceremony. There was a plate of steak for everyone.

'We didn't order steak,' Angela said.

'Only this meat,' said the safragi: 'All persons same. Very busy this place, this time.'

Simon knew that coming to Cairo had been a mistake. The men spoke of it as though life here was a perpetual carousal but to him it seemed a mad-house. Even the waiters were mad. When he learnt that Hugo was dead, he should have foregone his leave and returned to his unit. There, if he had nothing else, he had the comfort of familiar routine. The men would have understood how he felt but here no one understood or cared. But, of course, only two of them – Harriet Pringle and that odd, excitable woman called Lady Hooper – knew of Hugo's death. He looked at Harriet who, feeling his dejection, smiled at him and he smiled back, grateful that she had once had supper with Hugo and knew a little about him.

The table served, the Cherrypickers started up again. Discussing Queenie's favourite flower, they decided that it was a pansy. But was it a yellow or a white pansy?

Harriet was bored by the Cherrypickers yet scarcely knew with whom to ally herself. They were fighting men and, unlike Jackman, they were ready to risk their lives for others. Their trousers were purple-red in colour because – so the story went – in some early engagement, they had fought till the blood from their wounds flowed down to their feet. They could claim to have earned their amusement, but Cookson was poor game.

Moved to his defence, she said, 'Your jokes are so feeble. Can't we talk of something else?'

They gaped at her, silenced by their own astonishment, and Mortimer, looking at Harriet, nodded her approval. Feeling they were in sympathetic agreement, the two women began to talk to each other. Mortimer, Harriet discovered, was drowsy not from alcohol but from lack of sleep. She and a co-driver had driven to Iraq and back, taking it in turns to cat-nap so they could keep going through the night. This, she explained, was against regulations but gave them twenty-four hours of freedom when they got back. The co-driver had taken herself to bed but Mortimer had gone to the Semiris bar for a drink.

'Where I met these two blighters,' she said, yawning, damp-eyed with tiredness yet keeping awake from sheer cordiality.

'I envy you,' Harriet said: 'I was about to join the Wrens but got married instead.'

They talked about the days immediately before the war when there was no longer caution or pretence that a show-down could be avoided. Realising that war was inevitable, the English were united in a terrible excitement.

'We were all doomed, or thought we were,' said Harriet.

Mortimer asked, 'How did you get out here?' and Harriet explained that her husband, on leave, was ordered back to his lectureship in Bucharest. He and Harriet, having married in haste, travelled eastwards through countries mobilising troops and reached Bucharest on the day England entered the war.

Mortimer, at the same time, was embarking on a troopship for the Middle East. 'And I might have been with her,' Harriet thought, before she went on to explain how she and Guy had been evacuated to Greece and then to Egypt.

She asked, 'What is your first name?'

Mortimer, laughing and yawning at the same time, said, 'These days I have only one name. I'm Mortimer.'

The rich, red-brown of Mortimer's round face was set off by the periwinkle blue of her scarf, the privileged wear of a service that had once been voluntary and still had a scapegrace distinction.

'I suppose I wouldn't be allowed to join out here?' Harriet asked.

'No, there are no training facilities here.'

Angela said: 'You wouldn't qualify, darling. To get into Mortimer's outfit you have to be a lizzie or a drunk or an Irish-woman.'

Looking at Mortimer with her cropped hair, crumpled shirt and dirty cotton slacks, Harriet asked: 'Which are you?'

'Me? I drink.'

A small man had come on to the stage wearing white tie and tails. Clasping his hands before him like an opera singer, he opened his mouth but before he could make a sound, a man in the audience bawled: 'Russian.' This was immediately taken up and from all over the audience came a clamour of: 'Russian, Russian, Russian. We want Russian.' The performer threw out his hands in a despairing gesture, and Tony asked, 'What's all this about?'

Angela told him that the performer sang a gibberish which he could make sound like any language the audience chose, but he could not do Russian. The Cherrypickers, with expressions of concern, looked at each other and Terry said, 'Can't do Russian? M'deah, how queah!'

Jackman who had been silent, having no interest in any conversation but his own, now lost patience and said to Castlebar: 'A tedious lot, our wooden‑headed soldiery!'

Apparently not relating this remark to himself, Terry asked him: 'And what are you doing out here?'

'War correspondent.'

The Cherrypickers looked him over, noted his expression of baleful belligerency, and realising that picking on him would be much like picking on a hedgehog, they shifted their attention on to Castlebar who appeared less formidable.

'What do you do?'

'I‑I‑I'm a poet.'

The Cherrypickers collapsed together, clutching each other in an agony of mirth, while Castlebar, his threatening eye‑tooth showing on his lower lip, watched them from behind lowered lids. He was gathering himself to speak but Jackman got in first.

'I'm surprised two priceless specimens like you haven't come under the protection of BPHA.' He ran the letters together with an explosive spit that stopped the Cherrypickers in mid‑laugh.

'Come again?' Terry said.

'B‑P‑H‑A: Bureau for the Preservation of Hereditary Aristocracy. All the dukes, lords and what‑have‑yous are being brought back to base for their own safety. Too many of them wiped out in the First War. Can't let it happen again, can we?'

Terry looked perplexed: 'Is this true?'

'Of course it's true,' Jackman looked at Harriet: 'Your friend Lisdoonvarna's one of them.'

'Peter? He's moving heaven and earth to get back to the front.'

'Well, he won't get back. He'll be preserved whether he likes it or not.'

Having impressed everyone at the table, Jackman, slapping his hand down on his knee, sang at the top of his voice:

> Queen Farida, Queen Farida,
> How the boys would like to ride her . . .

The song had only three traditional verses but Jackman and Castlebar had added to them and as they increased in obscenity, people at neighbouring tables moved their chairs to stare at the singer and his companions. Then the Levantine manager, making a swift journey across the club floor, put a bill down in front of Jackman who came to an indignant stop.

The manager said, 'You pay. You go.'

'Go? Go where?'

'You go away. *Iggri.*'

'Like hell I will.'

Angela, picking up the bill, said, 'Yes, I think we will go.' As she took out her note-case, Jackman raged at her: 'Don't give them a cent. We'll miss the belly dance. If they turn us out, they can't make us pay . . .'

Angela, speaking with unusual quiet, said, 'Shut up. This isn't the first time we've been thrown out because of you. I'm getting tired of your behaviour.'

Jackman was thunderstruck by her severity and said nothing while she counted notes in a heap on to the bill. She let the Cherrypickers pay their share but when Simon tried to contribute, she put a hand over his and gently pushed the money away.

'Where now?' asked Castlebar.

Angela whispered in his ear. He grinned. 'Mystery tour,' she said. 'Come along,' and they all followed her out to the road. A row of taxis waited at the club entrance and Angela signalled to the first two. When they were seated, the others saw that Cookson had been left standing on the pavement. Angela beckoned to him but he shook his head and sadly wandered away.

She said: 'He's guessed where we're going. Not his cuppa.'

'Where *are* we going?' Mortimer asked.

'Wait and see.'

Harriet, too, guessed where they were going and had Simon showed any inclination to leave the party, she would have asked him to see her home; but he seemed bemused by everything about him and she did not wish to leave him alone among a crowd of indifferent strangers.

They seated themselves in the first taxi. Jackman, pushing in beside Mortimer, eyed her with lewd amusement: 'So you run around in a little lorry? And how do you spend your spare time?'

'We scrub out the ambulances that bring in the dead and wounded.'

'Nice work, eh?'

'Not very nice. The other day one of the girls, who had a cut in her hand, got gas gangrene.'

Scenting a story, Jackman sat up: 'What happened to her?'

'She died.'

Jackman sniffed and pulled at his nose while Harriet thought enviously: 'They belong to a world at war. They have a part in it: they even die,' but Harriet had no part in anything. She asked Mortimer which route they took to Iraq.

They tried to vary it, Mortimer said, but however they went, they had to cross the Syrian desert. Sometimes they headed straight for Damascus then turned east. Once they went to Homs so they could visit Palmyra but it had been a rough trip and they had broken a spring. Another time they went by the Allenby Bridge over the Jordan so they could see Krak de Chevalier.

'The Levant sounds wonderful. I'd love to go to Damascus.'

'We'd give you a lift. We're not supposed to, of course, but we often pick up people on the roads. The matron says it's dangerous but women alone are safer here than they are in England. We can thank Lady Hester Stanhope for that. She impressed the Arab world so every Englishwoman has a special status in those parts.'

'I wish I could go with you.'

Mortimer smiled at her enthusiasm: 'Any time.'

The taxis had taken them past the Esbekiya into Clot Bey where women stood in the shadows beneath the Italianate arches. From there they passed into streets so narrow that the pedestrians moved to the walls to enable the taxis to pass. No one, it seemed, needed sleep in this part of the city. Women looked out from every doorway. It was here that the squaddies came in search of enter-tainment and every café was alight to entice them in. Loud-speakers, hung over entrances, gave out the endless sagas relayed by Egyptian radio, while from indoors came the blare of nikol-odeons or player pianos thumping out popular songs.

As the taxis slowed down in the crowded lanes, beggars thrust their hands into the windows and small boys, leaping up and clinging to the framework, shouted: 'You wan' my sister? My sister very good, very cheap.'

Jake, putting his face close to them and mimicking their infant voices, shouted back: 'My sister all pink inside like white lady,' and the boys screamed with laughter.

The taxis reached a wider street where the women put their heads out of upper windows to importune the new arrivals. Some of them, leaning out too far, betrayed the fact that, richly dressed and bejewelled from the waist up, they were naked below. Jake began to sing: 'Greek bints and gyppo bints, all around I see, Singing "Young artillery man abide with me".' He gave Simon a sharp slap on the knee: 'You a young artillery man?'

Simon, bewildered, shook his head.

Angela asked him: 'Do you know where you are?'

Simon, who had been startled by the blow, looked out and asked, 'Is it the Berka?'

She laughed. 'The very place!' The taxis came to a stop in front of a house that looked like a small old-fashioned cinema. 'If there's anything to be seen, we'll see it here.'

The house front was bright with red and yellow neon and there was the usual uproar of Oriental and western music from inside and out; it suggested pleasure, but the pleasure-seekers, queuing outside, were an abject and seedy lot. A doorman controlled the queue and Castlebar was summoned from the second taxi by Angela to negotiate with him.

The English visitors watched as Castlebar and the doorman went down the line, the doorman speaking to each man in turn. Whatever he was trying to arrange did not meet with much response. At last a young man in trousers and crumpled cotton jacket, offered himself and was led away, downcast and down-at-heel, as though to his execution. Castlebar, returning, opened the door of Angela's taxi: 'All fixed up,' he said with satisfaction.

'What are they going to do with him?' Mortimer asked.

'He's the performer. In return, he'll get it for nothing.'

Holding to Simon as though fearing he would run away, Angela pushed him towards the door: 'Now, Sugar, out you get. What lots you'll have to tell the boys back in the desert.' She led the way into the house and the rest of the party, too befuddled to ask what was about to happen, followed. Harriet, knowing she would be safer inside than alone in the street with pimps, prostitutes and beggars, went with them. They were shown by a safragi into a downstair room where they stood close together, not speaking, transfixed by nervous curiosity. The room was hot and a smell of carbolic overlaid the resident smells of garlic and ancient sweat.

A half-negro woman, in a dirty pink wrapper, came in through a side door. Fat, elderly, bored and indifferent to the audience, she threw off the wrapper and lay on a bunk, legs apart.

One of the Cherrypickers whispered hoarsely: 'God, let's get out of here,' but he did not move.

The young man from the queue entered, wearing his shirt. He held his trousers in his hand and, giving the audience a sheepish glance, stood as though he did not know what to do next. The woman, having no time to waste, muttered, 'Tala hinna,' and held up her arms in a caricature of amorous invitation. The young man looked at her, then fell upon her. The union was brief. As he sank down, spent, she pushed him aside and, throwing the wrapper round her shoulders, made off on flat, grimy feet.

'Is that all?' Angela asked. She sounded defrauded but Simon felt they had more reason to feel ashamed.

The young man, left alone, was concerned to get back into his trousers. This done, he crossed to Castlebar, smiling his relief that the show was over. He said: 'Professor, sir, you do not know me, but I know you. At times I am attending your lectures.'

Castlebar began to stammer his consternation but unable to get a word out, offered the young man a cigarette.

Everyone, from a sense of chivalry, waited while cigarettes were smoked, then Angela, having given undue praise for the young man's performance, offered him a thousand piastre note.

'Oh, no, no,' he took a step back: 'I do not want. If it pleased you, that is enough.'

Castlebar, at last able to speak, asked him: 'Do you often give these performances?'

'No.' The young man looked dismayed by the question then, fearing he might seem impolite, excused himself: 'You see, we Egyptians are not like you Europeans. We are liking to do such things in private.'

'I think it's time to go,' Angela said. As they filed out, they each took the young man by the hand and murmured congratulations in an attempt to compensate him for the humiliation they had put upon him.

2

The taxis, taking them back, stopped first outside Shepaerd's where the Cherrypickers alighted, and Simon said: 'This will do for me, too.' As he thanked Angela and said his goodnights, Harriet asked if he would come to supper before his leave was up. He agreed to telephone her but it was a long time before she heard from him again.

The Cherrypickers were standing in front of the hotel. Imag-ining they would have no use for him he was turning to cross the road when Terry said, 'Come and have a last one.'

Surprised, taking it more as an order than an invitation, he went with them towards the hotel steps. Even at that hour, the life of the Esbekiya went on. Dragomen, in important dark robes, carrying heavy sticks, pursued the three officers, offering them: 'Special for you, many delights.'

'Thanks, we've just had them,' Terry said, raising a laugh among the people still sitting out at the terrace tables.

Inside, Simon saw by the hotel clock that it was past midnight and he felt himself delivered from the day that had passed. No other day, ever, at any time, could be as black as that day had been. He even felt reconciled to the Cherrypickers, realising they were not, as he had supposed, insufferably arrogant. Despite their splendid regiment and the advantage it gave them, they had, in fact, been challenged by the civilians and now, alone with him, they became simple and friendly.

He said to Terry, 'What did you think of the show, sir?'

'You mean that poor devil with the tart? I thought it pretty poor.'

Tony and Simon joined in agreeing with him and the three were united in their dislike of the exhibition. Simon was also reassured by the hotel interior which reminded him of the Putney Odeon. It was, no doubt, beyond his pocket but was not, as he had feared, beyond his dreams. The atmosphere, however, was disturbed, as though some catastrophe had taken place. Senior officers stood in the hall amid heaps of military baggage, drinking, but with an air of waiting expectancy.

Terry whispered to Tony, 'D'you think the balloon's going up? I'll mingle – see what's cooking.'

Simon watched respectfully as Terry moved among the officers looking for one of his own rank. He, himself, would not have dared to speak to any of them.

Returning, Terry said quietly, his face expressionless: 'Something's happening, all right, but they don't know what it is. Reconnaissance planes've seen preparations in the southern sector. Feeling is, jerry's all set for the big breakthrough.'

Tony permitted himself a little excitement: 'Then we'll be in at the kill?'

Simon, stuck in Cairo for a week, wondered if he would ever be in on anything. He had reached Suez during an emergency and been sent straight to the front amid the turmoil of an army that had been routed, or nearly routed. An army of remnants, someone called it.

He said, 'I suppose they had to break through sooner or later. I could see how thin our line was. I asked my CO why they didn't come on and he thought they just needed a rest.'

'Needed a rest? Like hell they needed a rest,' Terry said, 'I don't know how much action you've seen, old chap, but in our area we fought back and stopped the blighters in their tracks. That's why they didn't come on. We wouldn't give them another inch.'

'I see.' Simon spoke meekly, aware he had seen too little action to be any sort of judge of events. His sector, the great open tract south of the Ruweisat Ridge, was patrolled by mobile columns ordered to 'sting the jerries wherever and whenever they got the chance'. Simon, a junior officer in the dullest part of the line, had only once had a chance to sting anyone.

He said, 'When I was given leave, things seemed to be at a standstill.' He had imagined the whole line becalmed for ever in the treacle heat of summer and now, it seemed he had only to leave the desert for the war to come to life. Despondently, he said, 'My sector's south. Wish I was going with you.'

But why should he not go with them? His stay in Cairo, short though it was, had been a disaster. He wanted no more of it. At the thought of returning to the front, he rose for the first time since Hugo's death out of total desolation. To be in at the kill! To kill the killers! Everything else – Edwina's perfidy, the wretched party at the night club, the exhibition in the brothel – went from his mind and he eagerly asked: 'Can I come with you? I suppose you've got transport?'

'Yep, we managed to scrounge a pick-up. We could squeeze you in, but supposing it's only a twitch? You'd lose your leave for nothing.' Terry looked to Tony and laughed: 'If I had another week, I'd take it.'

Tony laughed, too: 'Leave doesn't come all that often!'

Simon did not explain his urgent desire to return to the desert but said, 'I'd be grateful for a lift.'

'OK. We're making an early start, so let's get that drink and call it a day.'

The Cherrypickers called for Simon at 06.30 hours next morning. Conditioned to rising at dawn, he was ready, waiting on the hotel steps. The pick-up, an eight-hundred-weight truck, was roomy enough. The three could travel in comfort.

The Cherrypickers had nothing to say that morning. Terry was at the wheel with Tony beside him. Neither had a word for Simon as he settled into the back with the baggage. He, for his part, knew he should speak only when spoken to, so they drove in silence through the empty streets in the pale morning sunlight.

The road out of Cairo was already a commonplace to Simon: the mud brick villas, the roadside trees holding out discs of flame-coloured florets, the scented bean fields, then the pyramids and the staring, blunted face of the sphinx. None of it stirred him now. He sank into a doze but outside Mena, where they ran into open desert, he was jerked awake as Terry braked to a stop. A man had been killed on the road. The body lay on the verge, wrapped in white cloth, and other men, workmen in galabiahs, seeing the truck approach, had run in front of it and held up their hands.

Terry shouted down to them, 'How'd it happen?'

The men, crowding round the truck, did not look very dangerous. Unable to understand the question, they glanced at each other then one said, 'Poor man dead', and from a habit of courtesy, grinned and put a hand over his mouth.

Saying, 'Oh, lord!' Terry put his fingers into his shirt pocket and pulled out some folded notes. Giving the man a pound, he said, 'For the wife and kids.' The spokesman, accepting it and touching his brow and breast in gratitude, waved to the others to let the truck through.

Driving on, Terry asked, 'What did you make of that?'

Tony laughed. 'Willing to wound and yet afraid to strike. They're easily bought off.'

'Fellow killed by an army lorry, I'd guess.'

Simon returned to sleep. Outside Alexandria, on the shore road near the soda lakes, Tony shook him awake, saying, 'How about brekker?'

The Cherrypickers had a picnic basket with them, packed by their hotel. The three men sat on the seaside rocks in the warm sea breeze. The food – portions of cold roast duck, fresh rolls, butter, coffee in a thermos flask – was far above the army fare to which Simon was used, but he was too self-conscious to express any opinion.

Terry asked, rather irritably, 'This all right for you?'

'I'll say. It's super.'

'Good. Thought perhaps you were tired of roast duck.'

'Never tasted it before.'

Simon was left to eat his fill while Terry and Tony discussed duck-shooting, a sport that was, they decided, carried to excess in diplomatic circles.

'Soon won't be a damned duck left,' Terry grumbled as he cleaned off a drumstick and started on a wing.

Tony gave him a sly, sidelong smile: 'Jolly nice, though, to have a bird in the fridge to pick at when you come in late.'

The meal finished, the Cherrypickers lay, eyes closed, in the sun while Simon, awaiting the order to move, threw stones into the slowly moving sea. At the eastern end of the shore road the traffic was light and the three men rested in a quiet that was almost peace. But the heat was growing and Terry, rousing himself, said, 'Better get underway.' For twenty miles or so he was able to keep a steady sixty miles an hour but reaching the forward area, they were slowed not only by trucks and cars but by infantry moving west.

Tony said, 'Certainly seems things are moving.'

When the sound of gunfire could be heard, Simon felt a familiar fear, yet, seeing about him the equipment of war, he had a sense of returning to the known world.

The petrol cans, set at intervals beside the road, indicated the direction of the different corps and divisions. None of this had relevance for the three men whose units were a good way south. Observing tanks in the distance, Terry raised his brows: 'Wonder what they're up to? Looks like training exercises.' A mile further on, he drew up by a supply dump and gave Simon a casual order: 'Care to go in and ask if they'll fill us up? Might get some gen while you're there.'

Dropping down off the back of the truck, Simon crossed to the wire enclosure. It was mid-day, the time of burning heat, and the smell of the dump hit him while he was several yards from it. The Column's signalman, Ridley, purveyor of scandals and rumours, had told him that food intended for the British civilians in Palestine was usually seized by the ordnance officers at Kantara: 'They take their whack and the rest goes into the blue to rot. Dead waste, I call it.' Ridley had no love for British officials but he had an acute dislike of ordnance officers who, he said, 'grow fat on what we don't get – which is proper grub.'

Admitted into the compound, Simon was directed to the command truck where he found the officer in charge at a desk beneath a lean-to. The stench trapped under the canvas was sickening but the officer, flushed and flustered, had other things to worry about. Hearing Simon approach, he said over his shoulder, 'What the hell do you want?'

'Petrol, sir.'

'Ah!' Simon's inoffensive request caused the officer to relax for the moment. Pushing back from the desk and wiping his face, he took out a cigarette: 'First today. Bloody circus here since that new chap took over.'

'We could see tanks in training. We wondered what was up.'

'It's the new chap, Monty they call him. He wants everyone fighting fit. Says he'll put 8th Army on its toes, so it seems things are hotting up.'

'There was a belief in Cairo that the show had started.'

'Not up here, it hasn't.'

'In the southern sector perhaps?'

'Could be. Nobody tells me anything.' The officer, not telling anything himself, took one more puff at his cigarette then squashed it into a tin where half-smoked cigarettes were twisted together like a nest of caterpillars. He stared about him, fearing some other demand would be made on him, but seeing only Simon, he lit another cigarette.

'Right. I'll give you a chitty then bring her in and fill her up. There'll be a Naafi truck round shortly if you feel like a snack.'

In mid-afternoon, Ruweisat Ridge appeared like a shadow through the fog of heat with immense clouds of dust rising and turning into the sky behind it. Tony said, 'Someone's getting it over there.'

Formations of Wellingtons were going south and Terry said with delight, 'We'll drive straight into it,' but a mile further on, when they had begun to feel the vibrations of heavy artillery, a military police car blocked the route and a policeman directed them to take a barrel track that ran eastwards, away from the battle.

Terry put up an angry protest: 'That's no good to us. We're not going that way. The 11th Hussars are down in Himeimat and we've got to join them.'

'No, sir, you must get on the track and stay on it. Himeimat's under heavy fire. Doubt if any of your chaps are left there now. You follow the track and you'll get to Samaket – if Samaket's still there.'

'If there's a barney on, we ought to be in it. If the Hussars are not at Himeimat, where are they?'

'Your guess is as good as mine, sir.'

Forced to turn eastwards, the three men grumbled at each other, disappointed yet excited. Terry said, 'We were almost in it – and now where are we going? It's like being chucked out of the theatre half-way through the show.'

In late afternoon the track, which had dropped south, brought them into a flat stretch of sand marked out with barrels to form enclosures for tank repair units, supply dumps, vehicle work-shops, dressing stations and mortuary huts. Simon had seen something similar in his early desert days and knew it was a depot for the battle in progress. They stopped at the command vehicle where a captain hurried towards them with the excited air of a man who brings good news. The enemy, he said, had attempted a breakthrough just north of Himeimat.

Terry struck the wheel in a rage: 'We've missed it. We've ruddy well missed it.'

The captain laughed. 'You haven't missed a thing.'

'Where are the jerries now, then?'

'Stuck in the mine fields.'

Terry swung round to face Tony: 'We must get in on this,' then asked the captain: 'You think they'll get any further?'

'There's no knowing. They've put in a fair bit of armour. Our reconnaissance reported a hundred or more Mark IIIs in the gap, but there's a storm blowing up. Dust so thick you can't tell sand from shit.'

In the general good fellowship, Simon found courage to enquire about his Column which he had left to the east of Ragil.

'What! Hardy's lot?' the captain gave a laugh that was almost a gibe: 'Last seen on the Cairo barrel track.'

'Not in action, I suppose?'

'Rather not. Seems like they were looking for rabbits.'

Simon jumped down from the pick-up. He could not get in on the fight and he had no excuse for staying with the Cherry-pickers. He must wait for a vehicle that would take him to wherever the Column was now.

As the hussars set off again, the captain shouted after them: 'Mind you don't drive straight into the bag.' He gave Simon a look and said, 'I've known that happen before now,' then, having nothing more to say to an inexperienced second lieutenant, he walked back to the command vehicle.

Simon carried his kit into the shade of a hut and sat down beside it. He could see the pick-up disappearing down the track in a cloud of dust. He envied the Cherrypickers but felt no regrets at parting with them. He had learnt independence during his months in the desert. In early days, he had attached himself to anyone who could, in some way, replace the lost relationships of home, but the need for those relationships had died as his friends died. He had become wary of affections that seemed always to end in tragedy. This last death, Hugo's death, had, he felt, brought his emotional life to a close. He no longer wanted intimates or cronies. He told himself he could manage very well on his own.

3

Dissatisfaction – chiefly Harriet's – was eroding the Pringles' marriage. Harriet had not enough to do, Guy too much. Feeling a need to justify his civilian status, he worked outside of normal hours at the Institute, organising lectures, entertainments for troops and any other activity that could give him a sense of purpose. Harriet saw in his tireless bustle an attempt to escape a situation that did not exist. Even had he been free to join the army, his short sight would have failed him. He thought himself into guilt in order to justify his exertions, and his exertions saved him from facing obnoxious realities.

Or so she thought. So thinking, she felt not so much resentment as a profound disappointment. Perhaps she had expected too much from marriage, but were her expectations unreasonable? Did all married couples spend their evenings apart? She felt that their relationship had reached an impasse but Guy was content enough. Things were much as he wanted them to be and if he noticed her discontent, it was only to wonder at it. He felt concern, seeing her too thin for health, but saw no reason to blame himself. He blamed the Egyptian climate and suggested she take passage on a boat due, some time soon, to sail round the Cape to England.

She had been dumbfounded by the suggestion. She would not consider it for a moment but said: 'We came together and when we leave, we'll leave together.' And that, she thought, decided that.

Guy seldom came in for meals and when he returned to the

flat one lunch⁄time, she asked with pleasurable surprise: 'Are you home for the rest of the day?'

He laughed at the idea. Of course he was not home for the rest of the day. He had come to change his clothes. He was to attend a ceremony at the Moslem cemetery and had to hurry. Harriet, following him to their room, said, 'But you will stay for lunch?'

'No. Before I go to the cemetery, I have to interview a couple of men who want to teach at the Institute.'

'So you're going to the City of the Dead?' Harriet was amazed. During their early days in Cairo, when he had had time to see the sights, he had rejected the City of the Dead as a 'morbid show', so what was taking him there now? He was going from a sense of duty. One of his pupils had been killed in a car accident and he was to attend, not the funeral, but the *arba'in*, the visit to the dead that ended the forty days of official mourning.

'Can I come with you?'

Guy, harassed by the need to dress himself all over again that day, said, 'No. It's probably only for men. But why not? It won't hurt them to be reminded that women exist. Yes, come if you like.'

He was a large, bespectacled, untidy man, now much improved by his well⁄cut dark blue suit, but he could not leave it like that. Stuffing his pockets with books and papers, he managed to revert to his usual negligent appearance, and becoming more cheerful, said, 'Meet me at Groppi's at three.'

'But will you *be* there at three?'

'Of course. Now, don't be late. I've a busy evening ahead, so we'll go early and leave early.'

As he left the room, she saw his wallet half out of his rear pocket and shouted, 'Put your wallet in before it gets nicked.'

'Thanks. Must hurry. Got a taxi waiting. Remember, don't be late. If you're late, I'll have to start without you.'

During September, the heat of summer had settled, layer upon layer, in the streets until they were compacted under a dead weight of heat which veiled the city like a yellow fog. Gropp's garden, a gravelled, open space surrounded by house walls and scented by coffee and cakes, was like a vast cube of Turkish delight.

Wandering into it at the sticky, blazing hour of three in the afternoon, Harriet saw that Guy was not there. She asked herself why had she ever thought he would be? He was always late yet his assurances were so convincing, she still believed he would come when he said he would.

Army men saw Groppi's as a good place for picking up girls and Harriet disliked being alone there. She had chosen a table close to the wall and felt herself to be an object of too much interest. She would, if she could, have hidden herself altogether.

The sun, immediately overhead, poured down through the cloth of the umbrellas like molten brass. Creepers, kept alive by water seeping from a perforated hose, rustled their mat of papery leaves. With nothing but creepers for company, she sat with downcast eyes and told herself she could murder Guy.

Someone said, 'Hello,' and, looking up, she saw Dobson had come to sit with her. They met at almost every meal time in the flat yet she welcomed him as a dear friend unseen for months and her spirits rose.

Dobson, as usual, had an amusing story to tell: 'They say things are so bad in Russia, they've started opening the churches. What I heard was: Stalin was driving out of the Kremlin one night and the headlights of his car lit a poster that said "Religion – the opium of the masses!" "My God," said Stalin, "That's just what we want these days: opium" and he ordered the churches to be reopened.'

'Did he really say "My God"?'

Dobson's soft sloping shoulders shook as he laughed: 'Oh, Harriet, how sharp you are!' he brushed a hand over his puffs of hair and asked, 'What would he say? He'd say "Oh, Russian winter!"'

'Really, Dobbie, you're ridiculous!'

By the time Guy arrived full of excuses and apologies, Harriet had forgotten her annoyance. When he asked if she had been waiting long, she replied blandly: 'Since three o'clock.'

He took this lightly: 'Oh, well, you had Dobbie.'

Although he had earlier emphasised the need to 'go early and leave early', he sat down and ordered tea, saying, 'I've just had the greatest piece of luck. Two chaps rang the Institute last week and said they wanted work, teaching English. I saw them today and – it's almost too good to be true – they're exactly what I've been looking for. They speak excellent English. They're well read, personable, willing to take on any number of classes. In fact, they're a gift. I think they could get much better paid jobs, but they want to teach.'

'Extraordinary!' said Dobson: 'What are they? Egyptians?'

'No, European Jews.'

'Called?'

'Hertz and Allain.'

Dobson, who expected to have knowledge of the European refugees under British protection, said, 'Never heard of them. What was their last place of residence?'

Guy had not thought to ask. 'Does it matter? They may have come from Palestine.'

'Did you ask what they are doing here?'

'No, but I suppose they can come here if they want to?'

'Why should they want to? Jews who have the luck to get into Palestine are only too glad to stay there.'

Not liking these questions, Guy became restless and looked at his watch. Gathering up his books, he said, 'It's gone four o'clock,' and added; 'I cannot see why you should be suspicious of two civilised, intelligent and harmless young men who want to teach. I can now delegate the English language classes and give my time to the literature.'

Never perturbed for long, Dobson smiled and said, 'Oh, well! But keep an eye on them in case . . .'

'In case of what?'

'I don't know. I just feel they're too good to be true.'

Guy glancing at Harriet, said, 'Darling, do hurry,' as though she were responsible for the hour. He had left a gharry waiting outside the café. When they were seated, he said to the driver, 'Qarafa,' and that was the first time Harriet heard the true name of the City of the Dead. He had learnt more Arabic than she had and was able to explain to the driver the dire need for haste. The man was so galvanised that he gave his horse a lick and the creature trotted for nearly a hundred yards before settling back into its usual lethargy.

They made their way through the old quarters of Cairo, among crowded streets from which minarets, yellow with sand, seemed to be crumbling against the cerulean of the sky. The kites, that found little of interest in the main roads, here floated, slow but keen-eyed, above the flat rooftops where the poor stacked their rubbish. As the lanes narrowed, the crowds became thicker and the enclosed air was filled with the smell of the spice shops. Guy, worried by their late arrival, had nothing to say.

Harriet, feeling the ride was spoilt by his mute disinterest in things, asked, 'Why didn't you come at three o'clock as arranged?'

'Because I had more important things to do. You don't stop to think how much I have on hand.'

His tone of controlled exasperation, exasperated her. 'Most of it unnecessary. I suppose you got so involved with the two teachers, you forgot the time.'

Truths of this sort annoyed him and he did not reply but stared ahead, his face creased as with suffering. 'This,' she thought, 'is marriage: knowing too much about each other.'

They came up to the Citadel wall and turned towards the desert region beneath the Mokattam Hills. At one time the dead had been buried in front of their homes, but Napoleon put a stop to that. Now they were carried up to their own city where there were streets and mausoleums built like houses. The relatives who escorted them took food and bedding and settled in until the spirit had become accustomed to the strangeness of the after life.

Harriet had thought this a pleasing idea until she learnt that the dead were not buried but merely placed under the floorboards on which the family had to sit. Having gone up with friends on moonlit excursions, when the place had a macabre attraction, she had once or twice caught a whiff of mortality that brought the imagination to a standstill.

Now, in the oppressive, fly-ridden heat of late afternoon, the city looked as discouraging as death itself. The air, reflected off the naked, cinderous Mokattam cliffs, was suffocating and Harriet said, 'I suppose we won't stay long?'

'No, it's just a courtesy visit.'

The gharry wheels sank into soft ground and the only noise in the dead streets was a snort from the horse. The driver asked where they wanted to go. Guy said the tomb belonged to a family called Sarwar; the dead boy was called Gamal. None of this meant anything to the man who went aimlessly between the rows of sham houses, some of which had sunk down into heaps of mud brick. The city seemed to be deserted but, turning into a main avenue, they came on a young boy standing alone. At the sight of the gharry, he took on joyful life and ran towards it.

'Ah, professor, sir, we knew you would come.' He was Gamal's brother, posted to intercept Guy, and had been waiting an hour or more. He jumped on to the gharry step and, talking excitedly, he explained that the *arba'in* went on all day so Guy must not think he was late. It was, of course, a family occasion but the Pringles must regard themselves as part of the family. And how welcome they were! Gamal who was, as it were, holding a reception to celebrate his inception into the next world, would be delighted.

Guy, though he did not believe in a next world, seemed equally delighted that his ex-pupil was now an established spirit.

A few streets further on, they came on the Sarwars gathered before the family tomb. It appeared to be, like most occasions in Egypt, an all-male function and Harriet said she would remain in the gharry. Gamal's brother would not hear of it. Mrs Pringle must join the party.

The Sarwar men, in European dress but each wearing his fez, stood in a close group, occasionally shaking hands or touching breasts with gestures of grief and regret. All this must have been done much earlier but now, to reassure the visitors, it was being re-enacted as though the Sarwars, like the Pringles, had just arrived.

Harriet was warmly received by the men who might keep their

own wives in the background but were quick to show pro-
gressive appreciation of an educated Englishwoman.

'Where is Madame Sarwar?' Harriet asked one of the men.

'Madame Sarwar?' he seemed for a moment to doubt whether
there was such a person, then he smiled and nodded. 'Madame
Sarwar Bey? She is, naturally, with the other ladies.'

'And where are the other ladies?'

'They are together with Gamal in the house.'

Glancing inside the tomb, she saw dark forms in the darkness
and, imagining the hot, crowded room with the corpse beneath
the floorboards, she was thankful that no one suggested she
should join them.

But something was required of Guy. After they had exchanged
condolences and compliments, Sarwar Bey, a stout man in youthful
middle-age, took Guy by the arm and led him close to the tomb,
beckoning Harriet to follow. The other men came behind them
and they all stood at a respectful distance gazing into the door
from which the black-clad women retreated.

Taking Guy a step forward, Sarwar Bey called to his son:
'Gamal, Gamal! Emerge at once and witness who is among us.'
He paused, then satisfied that Gamal had obeyed his command,
he shouted vigorously: 'My boy, who do you see? It is your
teacher, Professor Pringle, come to visit you on your *arba'in*. This
is a very great honour and on your behalf I will tell him you are
very much pleased.' This admonitory oration went on for some
time, then Sarwar Bey turned to address Guy.

'And you, Professor Pringle, you will remember our Gamal
for a long time, even when you have gone back to England.
Isn't that so, Professor Pringle?'

Sarwar Bey spoke impressively and Guy was impressed. Tears
stood in his eyes and at the final words, he gulped and put his face
into his hands. The Egyptians, emotional people who warmed to
any display of emotion, crowded round him to console him by
pressing his arm or patting his back or murmuring appreciation.
Sarwar Bey, holding him by the shoulder, led him away from
the house and wept in sympathy.

A woman servant came from within carrying cups of Turkish

coffee on a large brass tray. This strong restorative was pressed on Guy who, making a swift recovery, became the vivacious centre of the group of men.

Harriet, remaining apart, watched the men making much of Guy who beamed about him, enjoying the attention and recalling things said and done by Gamal. Gamal, he said, had written in an essay: 'My professor, Professor Pringle, is an Oriental. But if he is not, he should be because he is one of us!'

Gamal may have said that, or written it. Certainly some one had said it: and in Rumania and Greece there were people who had said the same thing. They had all laid claim to him and he had responded. He was, Harriet felt, disseminated among so many, there was little left for her.

The evening was coming down. The heat fog was turning to umber and through it the lowering sun hung, a circle of red-gold, above the western river bank that had been the burial place of the ancient dead.

The gharry horse stamped its feet and Harriet shared its bored weariness. She was depressed by the arid inactivity of the cemetery and wished them away. Then, as the light changed, the scene changed and she was entranced by it. The white Mohammed Ali mosque, that squatted like a prick-eared cat on the Citadel, took on the roseate gold of the sky and everything about it – the Mokattam cliffs, the high Citadel walls, the small tomb houses – glowed with evening. As the heat mist cleared, she could see in the distance the elaborate tombs of the Caliphs and Mamelukes, and thought that as they had driven so far, they might drive a little further and see the Khalifa close to.

The colours faded and twilight came down. Inside the Sarwar house, the women had lit petrol lamps and the flames flickered in the unglazed windows. The Khalifa tombs ceased to be visible but as the moon rose, they reappeared, touched in by a line of silver light.

Guy, eager enough to stay among his admirers, had to realise that time was passing. It was almost dark. The last day of mourning was coming to an end. The Sarwars themselves would soon

49

return home and Gamal would be left alone. One after the other, the men took Guy by the hand and held to him a little longer than necessary as though, for a while, he could deliver them from the bewildering inexpedience of life.

Then they had to let him go. As he followed Harriet to the gharry, she pointed to the Khalifa monuments edged with moon light: 'Let's go and look at them.'

'Good lord, no. Who would want to see things like that?'

'They're magnificent. And they're no distance away.'

'Sorry, but I'm late as it is. I have to get to the Instiute. You can go any time to see them. Ask Angela to go with you.'

'But I want to go with you.'

'Darling, don't be unreasonable. You know how I hate things like that. Useless bric-à-brac, death objects, *memento mori*! What point in making oneself miserable?' He climbed into the gharry.

Harriet stood where she was, watching the moon that heaved and rippled like liquid silver through the moisture on the horizon. Then, rising clear, it shed a light of diamond whiteness that picked out the traceries of the great tombs and lit the small houses of the common dead so that the cemeteries, arid and dreary during the day, became mysterious and beautiful.

Guy, losing patience, called to her and they drove down into the old streets where the mosques lifted themselves out of shadows into the pure indigo of the upper air. The evening star was alone in the sky but before they reached the main roads, the sky was ablaze with stars, all brilliant so the evening star was lost among them. This time of the evening, Harriet felt, compensated for the heat and glare, the flies and stomach upsets of the Egyptian summer. Her energy was renewed and feeling reconciled to Guy, she put her hand on his and said, 'Darling, don't be cross.'

He said, 'Have you thought any more about taking the boat to England.'

She withdrew her hand: 'No, I haven't thought any more because I'm not going. I don't want to hear any more about it.'

She had told him the question was settled and his bringing it up again when she was affectionate and, he supposed, compliant, gave evidence of his obstinacy and his cunning. These qualities, known only to her, were seldom manifested but when manifested, irritated her beyond bearing.

Neither spoke again until they came into the wide, busy roads with large pseudo-French buildings, shabby and dusty during the day but coming alive at night when windows lit up, and there were glimpses of rooms where anything might be happening. Pointing to some figures moving behind lace curtains, Harriet said, 'What do you think is going on in there?'

Guy shook his head. He did not know and did not care. He seemed distant and vexed, and she felt this was because she had refused to go on the boat to England. The thought came into her head: 'He wants me to go because he wants me out of the way.' But why should he want her out of the way?

When they came to the Institute, he left her to take the gharry on to Garden City. 'I won't be late,' he said and Harriet said, 'It doesn't matter. I'll probably be in bed before you return.'

She thought, 'If I go, it will be because I want to go. And if I don't want to go, I won't go. And if he has any reason for wanting me to go, I don't care, I don't care, I don't care.'

She looked defiantly at the crowded, brilliant street where everyone seemed intent on enjoyment, and she wondered, miserably, what reason she had for staying with a husband she seldom saw in a place where she had no real home and little enough to do.

4

Reaching the Column five days sooner than he was expected, Simon was aware of ridicule rather than approbation. When he reported his return to Major Hardy, the major said fretfully: 'What brings you back at this time, Boulderstone?'

'I thought you'd want me here, sir. In Cairo, they're all saying the balloon's going up.'

Hardy, his dark, lined face contracting as though he were in intense pain, seemed at a loss. He had been headmaster of a small school, and no doubt had been happy in his power, but the war had disrupted his life and he had manoeuvred himself, from vanity, into a position beyond his capacity. Simon, who had gathered this partly from Ridley and partly from his own observation of the man, saw now that his unnecessary return had upset Hardy by exceeding the natural order of things.

'I'm sorry, sir.'

'All right, Boulderstone.' Reassured by the apology, Hardy spoke more kindly: 'It's as well you're here. No knowing what will happen. Something could be underway, though I've heard nothing.'

Ridley, finding Simon back in camp, could hardly hide his derision. 'You handed in five days, sir? Back to the old grind for sweet damn all? Well, I hopes the night you was there, you didn't waste no time.'

Simon was able to say with truth: 'I went to the Berka.'

'You didn't!' Ridley's face, burnt to the colour of an Arbroath smokie, was cut through by his lascivious smile: 'Well, good for you, sir!' He whistled his appreciation and said nothing more about the wasted five days. That evening, when they were supervising a brew-up, he asked Simon: 'Find the captain all right, sir?'

'The captain?'

'That captain you went to look up? The one you thought might be your brother?'

As Simon shook his head and walked away, Ridley called after him: 'Not the right bloke, then, sir?' but Simon pretended not to hear.

The battle at Himeimat was in its third day before the Column came within sound of it. Ridley, in touch with the news and rumours of the line, brought what he heard to Simon.

He said, 'The jerries've been taking a pasting. They were stuck all day in the mine fields with our bombers belting hell out of them and our tanks waiting to blast them when they got out.'

'And did they get out?'

'Don't know. Better ask his nibs.' Ridley jerked his head towards the HQ truck where Hardy, standing on a seat with his head through a hole in the roof, was observing the westward scene through his over-large binoculars.

Simon went to him: 'See anything, sir?'

He was risking a snub because Hardy, inclined to self-importance, preferred to keep his information to himself. This time, surprisingly, he replied with unusual friendliness: 'Not much. Plenty of smoke from burning vehicles but no sign of the hun.' Putting down the binoculars, he turned to smile on Simon who flushed, feeling a fondness for the man.

The Sunday after his return to the unit had been declared a national day of prayer: Monty's idea. Ridley said: 'They say he's a holy Joe. Thinks he's got a direct line to God.'

The padre arrived in a staff car and a squaddy set up a small portable altar in the sand. Going into the HQ truck, the padre was affable and smiling. Coming out, wearing his cassock, he was grave-faced and he made an authoritative gesture to the congregation of men seated cross-legged, awaiting him. They stood up for the hymn, 'Now praise we all our God'. The singing began but the battle did not stop. During the night the flashes and flares on the horizon, and the near gunfire, had kept the camp in a state of semi-wakefulness. Now, as the loud but tuneless praise went forth, it was drowned by flights of Wellingtons overhead.

Ridley whispered behind Simon: 'Still giving the buggers hell.'

A new distraction arrived during prayers. A messenger on a motor-cycle drew up beside the group of officers and waited until Hardy, head bent, put out a hand for the signal. Opening it, still muttering his devotions, he appeared to be thunderstruck by what he read. His prayers ceased and, looking up, he stared at Simon in furious astonishment. Simon, his conscience clear, glanced uneasily round at Ridley who shrugged his ignorance of the contretemps. As soon as the padre had driven off to another camp, Hardy's batman called Simon to the HQ truck.

'Any idea what's wrong?'

'Haven't a clue, sir.'

As Simon approached the truck, Hardy, seated at an outdoor table, observed him with black indignant eyes, saying as soon as he was within earshot: 'So, Boulderstone, you have friends in high places?'

'Me, sir! I don't know anyone.'

'Well, someone appears to know you. Or know *about* you. Your fame has spread beyond the Column – can't think why. I, myself, failed to recognise your superior qualities, but the fault no doubt was mine.'

Hardy went on at length until Simon, baffled and miserable, broke in: 'I'm sorry, sir, but I don't understand any of this.'

'No? Well, you're to leave us, Boulderstone. The Column is to be deprived of your intelligence and initiative. We must somehow manage without you. Its activities are obviously too limited for a man of your resource and vision.'

Simon, by remaining silent, at last brought Hardy to the point. 'You've landed, God knows how, one of the most sought-after jobs in the British army. For some reason hidden from me, someone has seen fit to appoint you a liaison officer.'

As Hardy spoke the memory of Peter Lisdoonvarna came to Simon and he murmured, 'Good heavens!' never having imagined that the social chat in the Garden City flat had meant anything at all.

Simon began, 'I did meet a chap in Cairo . . .' then came an embarrassed stop. It must seem that he had, ungratefully, sought a transfer behind the back of his commanding officer and he tried to explain.

Hardy refused to listen: 'I don't know how you managed it, and I don't want to know. You've got the job. Whether you're fit for it or not is another matter. It's none of my concern. It'll be up to you, Boulderstone, to prove yourself.'

'Sir! Where am I to go, sir?'

'You'll hear soon enough. They're sending a pick-up for you and you'll be taken to Corps HQ. The driver will bring your instructions. And I'd advise you to clean yourself up. Get your shirt and shorts properly washed. At Corps HQ, you'll be among the nobs.'

The other officers of the Column showed that they shared Hardy's disapproval of Simon's advancement and it was also shared by Ridley. Ridley who in early days had been Simon's guide and support, now avoided him and was vague when Simon sought him out to question him. What, Simon wanted to know, were the duties of a liaison officer?

'Don't worry, sir. You'll find out for yourself. You'll soon cotton on.'

'You don't think I'm up to it, do you?'

'It's not for me to say, sir. With respect, I'd rather not discuss it. I've got to be getting along.'

Simon, unnerved at leaving the safety of the Column, felt an impulse to stay where he was but knew that the appointment came when he most needed it. He was sick of the tedium of eventless patrols. Opportunity to escape was offered and he would not be restricted by the disapprobation of other men.

Still, he was troubled. Hardy's annoyance came of Hardy's vanity, but Ridley was another matter. Ridley was hurt by his going and this hurt resulted from affection, even love. In the desert where there were no women or animals, Ridley had to love something and he had chosen Simon. Simon was touched, but not as deeply as he would once have been. His own attachments – Trench on the troopship which brought them to Egypt, Arnold his batman and driver, and Hugo – were dead and their deaths had absolved him from overmuch feeling. He was sorry to leave Ridley, but no more than that.

The transport, which arrived two days later, was not a pick-up but a jeep. The jeep had been assigned to Simon, it was his own vehicle, and this fact, when Hardy and the others heard of it, confirmed them in their belief that Simon had been appointed above his station. They were short with their goodbyes but the men, crowding about him as he prepared his departure, showed genuine regret at his going. They liked him. Only Ridley did not join in their good wishes but stood at a distance. When Simon shouted to him, 'Goodbye, Ridley, thanks for everything,' he dropped his head briefly, then walked away. When, starting out, Simon looked back to wave, the men waved him away but there was no sign of Ridley.

For a mile or so Simon was sunk in sadness, then the Column and everyone in it dwindled behind him and he felt the exhilaration of a new beginning. He looked at the driver and asked his name.

'Crosbie, sir.'

'You attached to me permanently?'

'Yes, sir.'

Crosbie, lumpish, snub-faced, with a habit of smiling to himself, showed no inclination to talk but drove with the stolid efficiency of a man who did one, and only one, thing well. He could drive.

They passed the Ridge, almost lost in the dusty haze, and turned on to a barrel track. The track took them eastwards beyond the sound of the guns into the spacious, empty desert where the only danger was from the air. Relaxing from his usual attentive fear, Simon faced the challenge of the work awaiting him. He would have liked to question Crosbie about the corps, but his instinct was to keep himself to himself.

He had started his desert life under Hardy and had relied on Arnold and Ridley. These two NCOs, taking pity on his ignorance, had pampered him as though he were a youngster, but he had tried Hardy's patience and Hardy saw him as a fool. Well, that episode was over. Simon now had experience of the desert, and no one would treat him either as fool or youngster.

The horizon lightened as they approached the coast. There were aircraft about and Simon, seeing one of them rise, leaving in the distance a long trail of ginger-brown dust, asked from an old habit of enquiry: 'Where's that taking off from?'

Crosbie, not bothering to look at it, mumbled, 'Don't know, sir!' Neither knowing nor caring, he was not one to answer questions and Simon decided that he would no longer be the one to ask them.

They reached the perimeter of Corps HQ in the early afternoon. Passing concentrations of trucks and equipment, and all the appurtenances of operational and administrative staff, Simon was awed by the extent of the camp. But this was where he now belonged. Its size denoted his status in the world. When the jeep jerked to a stop, they had reached the dead end of a lane and Crosbie said, 'This doesn't look right, sir.'

Simon brusquely replied: 'Get your finger out, Crosbie. You're supposed to know where you're going. The command vehicle is posted. Use your eyes.'

Crosbie might well have pointed out that Simon had eyes and could use them but, instead, he acknowledged authority with a brisk 'Sir', and backing the jeep out of the lane, brought them at last to the busy centre of the camp.

Simon was not the only new arrival. The command vehicle, a three-ton truck converted for use as an office, had a canvas lean-to, camouflaged with netting that extended on both sides. A number of officers, all senior to Simon, stood in groups under the lean-to awaiting the attention of the officer in charge. They talked with the flippant ease he had admired in the Cherry-pickers and he saw them as old campaigners to whom the desert was a second home.

Simon, who had been oppressed by Hardy's doubts and uncertainties, now felt his spirits rise as he listened to these men who had no doubt at all that, whatever happened, the allies would be the victors in the end.

The officer in charge was a major, verging on middle-age, with a thin, serious face, who tolerated the chaffing of the other men but did not respond to it. Simon, when his turn came, expected no more than an acknowledgement of his arrival, but the major, who said, 'I'm Fitzwilliams. You'll take your orders from me,' looked at him with interest and afforded him several minutes of his time.

'I'm afraid, Boulderstone, you've reached us just when the chaps are moving up from their training grounds. A deal of armour will be coming in and you'll find it a bit confusing at first, but you'll soon know your way around. Don't be frightened to ask. You're in B mess so you can go along now and get yourself a snack. Report back here at 23.00 hours. I'll probably have a job for you.'

Simon, sitting under the canvas lean-to that was B mess, wondered if he had heard right. To the men of the Column, 23.00 hours was in the middle of the night. Was he expected to start work at a time when other men were fast asleep? All he could do was report at the hour given and hope he was not making a fool of himself.

Twenty-three hours, it turned out, was the expected arrival time of an armoured division and Simon was sent to conduct the tank commander to the correct assembly point. Where that point was, Simon had to find for himself and, returning to the jeep, he said casually to Crosbie: 'I suppose you know the assembly point for tanks?'

Crosbie, who obviously did not, mumbled 'Sir' and, setting out, stopped to enquire at every hut and bivouac that showed a light. The commander had found the assembly point long before the jeep reached it but Simon did not betray himself.

'Just been sent, sir, to see you've settled in.'

'Yep, all in. All tickety-boo.'

Thankful to have skirted this assignment safely, Simon relented towards Crosbie and said, 'That wasn't too bad. Now let's hope we can get some kip,' but their night's work was not yet over. Reporting back to the command vehicle, Simon found a different officer in charge. He said, 'You're the new liaison officer, are you? Well, I've got a job for you. D'you know the compound with the dummy lorries? No? I expect you'll find it easily enough. Look out the ordnance officer and give him a signal: he's to fit the dummies over the newly arrived tanks.'

'When, sir? Tomorrow?'

'No, not tomorrow. Everything here happens at night. The job's to be done before first light. Now, get a move on.'

An hour later, having tracked down the ordnance officer, Simon apologetically handed him the signal: 'I'm sorry, sir, but it's supposed to be done before daybreak.'

Amused by his tone, the officer looked at Simon, smiled and nodded: 'Received and understood,' he said.

Free now to sleep, Simon ordered Crosbie to park near the command vehicle in order to be on call. Then, Simon in his sleeping-bag, Crosbie on his ground-sheet, they dossed down on either side of the jeep.

The assembly of the camp was growing and from its proportions, Simon realised that the purpose behind it was not merely defensive. And, as he had been told, everything happened at night. The convoys and units journeyed in darkness, and in darkness took up their positions in the camp. This, he knew, would not happen on a routine training march.

Dummy equipment was collected in dumps and mysteriously moved about. He found, when delivering signals, that the dummy guns and vehicles of yesterday had been replaced by real guns and vehicles, or the real had been replaced by dummies. The purpose was to deceive, and the deceived could only be the enemy. Simon would have been glad to have Ridley with him to make sense of all this shifting and replacement. Several times he almost asked Crosbie, 'What's going on?' but kept quiet, seeing no reason for wasting words.

As Fitzwilliams had promised, he soon knew his way around but he suffered from a lack of companions. Two other liaison officers were due and, sitting alone in B mess, he longed for their arrival.

The heat had dragged on into mid-September, and seemed, to tired senses, more exhausting than summer. Under the tarpaulin the air was turgid with food smells and singed by the cooks' fires. Simon was dulled by inactivity and the atmosphere, when another liaison officer came to join him. This was Blair, a captain, and Simon, standing up, said, 'Glad you've come, sir.'

Blair laughed with the uncertainty of a man who has lost his place in the world: 'Just call me Blair.'

He was soft-bodied, stoutish, puffy about the cheeks and eyes, and his hair was growing thin. Simon thought him a very old fellow to be living among the hardships of the desert. He was not the companion Simon had hoped for, but any companion was better than none.

Blair sat with Simon at meal times but had little to say for himself. When he was not eating, he would sit with his head down, his hands hanging loosely between his knees. He had been in tanks and wore the black beret, but not with pride. Whenever he could, he would take it off and fold it into his pocket.

The third liaison officer, when he turned up, had no more to offer than Blair. His name was Donaldson and although the same age as Simon, he had finished his year as a second lieutenant. With two pips up, he was able to treat Simon as an inferior. He tried at first to come to terms with Blair, but finding him sad company, he ignored both his fellow liaison officers and sat by himself.

Blair, after a few days, began to talk. Hesitant and nervous, he said he had served in the desert since the first year of the war. In those days, with only the Italians to contend with, it had been 'a gentleman's war'. His CO had said that here in the desert, they had a 'soft option', but then the Afrika Korps had arrived to spoil things. By hints, pauses and a shaking of the head, he made it clear that some unnatural catastrophe had struck him down near a place he called Bir Gubo. 'East of Retma', he said as though that meant anything to Simon. Blair mentioned other names: Acroma, Knightsbridge, Adem, Sidi Rezegh, which all, for Simon, belonged to the era of pre-history when the British still operated on the other side of the wire that marked the Egyptian frontier.

'With all that armour round you, you must have felt pretty safe?'

Blair's eyes fixed themselves on Simon: 'Safe? You ever seen inside one of those Ronsons after it's burnt out?'

'Not inside, no.'

'Imagine being packed inside a tin can with other chaps and then the whole lot fried to a frizzle. What do you think you'd look like?' Blair gave a bleak laugh and Simon said no more about tanks.

Instead, he wiped the sweat off his face and asked Blair, 'Does it ever let up?'

'I've known worse summers, but not one that lasted into October.'

October came. As though the change of month meant an automatic change of weather, the hard, hot wind stopped abruptly and a softer wind came cool out of the east and dispersed the canteen's flies. The nights became colder and jerseys were regulation wear. Those officers who owned sheepskin coats, now wore them swinging open so the long, inner fleece hung out like a fringe.

Hardy, ordering Simon to clean himself up, had said, 'You'll be among the nobs,' but 'the nobs' were much less conventional in dress than Hardy and his staff. Hardy himself always wore a carefully knotted tie but the officers at Corps HQ wore silk scarves, rich in colour, and their winter trousers of corduroy velvet – khaki and serge, apparently, were for other ranks – could be any colour from near-white to honey brown. That had for Simon a swaggering elegance and he greatly envied them. He told Blair that when he was next in Cairo he would buy some corduroy trousers and a sheepskin coat.

'Be careful about the coat,' Blair said. 'Those skins can stink to high heaven if they're not properly cured. Often, with all the smells in the Muski, you don't notice it till you get it home. If you try to return it, the chap who sold it can't be found. I had a fine Iranian coat once, best skins, embroidered all over. Was sorry to lose it.'

'You mean someone liberated it?'

'No, lost it at Bir Gubo. Lost a lot of things.'

'What *did* happen at Bir Gubo?'

Blair, biting into a bully-beef sandwich, tried to smile with his mouth full. He chewed and coughed and managed to say, 'You mean, to the coat? Got burnt.'

'Not just the coat. You and the rest of the crew? – what happened?'

Blair cleared his mouth with a gulp of tea. 'They bought it – all except me. I'd gone for a walk . . . You know, with a spade. Heard a plane go over. Didn't see it. Didn't even know whose it was. When I got back the Ronson was ablaze. Couldn't get near it. We'd been fart-arsing around, not a soul in sight. Must've taken a direct hit. I don't know. Simply don't know. I just stood there and watched till it burnt out . . . And when I went to look, you couldn't tell one chap from another.'

'And what happened to you?'

'Don't know. Wandered about . . . shock, I suppose. The Scruff found me and thought I was dead. Just going to bury me when someone saw my eyelids move. Just a twitch, as the chaps say. Saved my life.' Blair laughed so his tea cup shook in his hand, and Simon felt he knew all he need know about Blair's descent from a tank's officer to a messenger who carried signals for other men.

Simon asked him, 'Any idea what's happening here? There's a mass of stuff coming in. Do you think it's the attack?'

'Could be. Certainly looks like it.'

'When will it be, do you think?'

'Have to be soon. There's the moon, you see. And you can't keep a show like this sitting on its arse. The jerries might see it and strike first. There'll be a showdown all right.'

'You looking forward to it?'

'Don't know. Perhaps. Better than hanging about.'

The moon was growing towards the full and expectations grew with it. In the middle of the month, when anything might happen, Simon was sent south towards the point at which he had parted from the Cherrypickers. Of the big supply base, not a barrel remained but a small force of camouflaged tanks were, hull down, in the wadi where the command lorry had stood. The officer in charge was lying on high ground, looking westwards through field glasses. When Simon came to him, bringing a movement order, he said in a low voice, 'Get down.' Simon crouched beside him and he pointed to a bluff of rock distorted by the mid-day heat: 'See over there; that's the salient. They've been there since Alam Halfa. If you listen, you can hear them singing.'

Lying down, Simon bent his head to extend his hearing and there came to him, faint and clear, like a voice across lake water, a song he had heard somewhere before: 'But that's an English song!'

'No, it's one of theirs: "Lili Marlene". We picked it up from the German radio.'

The two men, lying side by side, remained silent while the song lasted. Simon, moved by its nostalgic sadness, thought of the first time he had seen Edwina. She had leant over the balcony towards him, her face half-hidden by a fall of sun-bleached hair, her brown arm lying on the balcony rail, her white robe falling open so he could see the rounding of her breasts. She came back to him so vividly, he thought he could smell her gardenia scent. He was impatient of the vision and relieved when the song ended and the officer, laughing and jumping up, said, 'So we're to take the tanks up north? Gathering us all in, eh? Looks like things are hotting up?'

'We hope so, sir. The signal says: "Move only after dark".'

'Will do. Received and understood.'

As Simon drove back, Edwina was still on his mind. He tried to order her away but she stayed where she was, smiling down on him from the balcony. The desert air was a sort of anaphrodisiac, and he and the other men were detached from sex, yet he could not reject the romantic enhancement of love. He took out his wallet to distract himself, and, opening it, looked for the photograph of his wife. He could not find it. He could not even remember when he had last seen it. At some time during the past weeks, perhaps during the last months, it had fallen out, and now it was lost. He tried to recreate her in his mind but all he could see was a thin, small figure standing, weeping, on the station platform. She had no face. He struggled with his memory but no face came to him and he wondered, were he to meet her unexpectedly, would he know who she was?

5

In October, when the evenings grew cool, Dobson ordered the servants to take blankets out of store. A smell of moth-balls filled the flat as he distributed them, saying again and again: 'So delicious to have a bit of weight on one at night.'

The Garden City foliage scarcely marked the change of season. A few deciduous trees, hidden among evergreens and palms, dropped their leaves. These went unnoticed but one tree – the students called it the Examination Tree – made a dramatic appearance out of nowhere, feathering its bare branches with mauve blossom, mistaking the autumn for spring.

The morning air became gentle as silk and a delicate mist hung over the old banyans on the riverside walk. The heat, that had dulled the senses like a physical pressure, now lifted and minds and bodies felt renewed. Lovers, no longer suffering the wet and sticky sheets that were cover enough during the summer, became invigorated: and the one most invigorated, it seemed, was Castlebar.

The inmates of the flat were astonished when Angela first led him through the living-room to her bedroom where they remained closeted all afternoon. Castlebar, on his way out, passed Harriet and Edwina with a very smug smile. Angela, appearing later for her evening drink, was not discomposed and made no comment on Castlebar's visit. The next day he was back again.

Edwina, who had not seen Castlebar before, said to Harriet, 'Where did Angela pick up that scruffy old has-been?'

Harriet could not believe the infatuation would last, but it was lasting and becoming more fervent. Castlebar was with Angela every afternoon. She confided to Harriet that the keeper of the cheap pension where Castlebar lived had objected to her presence in Castlebar's room. The woman had demanded double payment for what she called, 'the accommodation of two persons'. Angela would have paid the required sum but Castlebar argued that he had a right to bring in a friend. He said he would not be cheated by 'a greedy Levantine hag' and they settled the matter by changing ground.

Harriet and Angela were neighbours in the bedroom corridor and Harriet overheard more than she wanted of the chambering next door. She had no hope of a siesta and went to the living-room to read in peace. Dobson, whose room was in the main part of the flat, once or twice wandered out, a towel, tied like a sarong round his waist, and realising why Harriet had retreated, shook his head over Angela's fall from grace.

'The goings-on!' he grumbled after they had been going on for a week: 'To think she would take up with a shocker like Castle-bar! And I'm told he's got a wife somewhere. What does she see in him?'

Harriet tried to imagine what Angela saw in him. In the picture that came to her mind, Castlebar, worn down by self-indulgence, middle-age and the Egyptian climate, had a folded yellow skin and a mouth that looked unappetisingly soft, like decayed fruit.

She shook her head: 'I don't know. But what does anyone see in anyone? Perhaps that's what Yeats meant by "love's bitter mystery"!'

Dobson, though he had never objected to Peter Lisdoon-varna's presence in Edwina's room, said he meant to be firm with Angela. 'It's going too far. You might drop her a word. Tell her I don't like it'.

When Harriet attempted to drop the word, Angela broke in to ask, 'What has it got to do with him? Perhaps he wants me to pay double expenses?'

'Angela, you're being disingenuous. He feels that Castlebar's not worthy of you – he debases you socially.'

The two women laughed and Harriet felt it best to avoid Dobson and his complaints. A few afternoons later, keeping to her room, she was startled by a ringing crash followed by Castlebar's half-stifled snuffling titter. After he had gone, Harriet, passing Angela's open door, found her on her knees, mopping water from the floor.

'Sorry if we disturbed you.'

'I didn't hear a thing.'

'Bill knocked down a dish of water. He keeps it by the bed because he's inclined to come too soon so, when he's over excited, he dips his wrist in the water and it cools him down.'

This explanation, unblushing and matter-of-fact, took for granted Harriet's acceptance of the situation and she could only say, 'I see.'

'And you can tell bloody Dobson that Bill won't be here much longer. He's found himself a flat.'

'He's been very clever. When we wanted one, we couldn't find a thing.'

'The situation's easier now as some of the officers are going. And the university has a few flats for its men. Bill put his name down for one as soon as he heard his wife was determined to get back. He had to. He said if he didn't stir himself on her behalf, she'd raise hell.'

'You mean, he's frightened of her?'

'Terrified. Poor Bill!'

Angela smiled in amused contempt, and yet the enchantment remained. Their afternoons together were not enough for her, she had to see him again in the evening. If, by chance, they had not made an arrangement to meet later, she would go to the Union in search of him, always taking Harriet with her. She was generous with her friends who, in return, were required to support her in her caprices.

Now that the nights were growing cold, the Union members were retiring from the lawn into the club house and there Angela chose a corner table and held it as her own. The chief safragi, heavily tipped, would place an 'Engaged' notice on the table and there she would sit for as long as need be, awaiting Castlebar.

Her friends were not the only ones to marvel at her intimacy with him. When he appeared, as he did sooner or later, those sitting around would glance askance at the two of them and then at each other.

None of this worried Angela and Castlebar, who openly held hands, Castlebar cleverly manipulating his cigarette and drink with his right hand while his left kept its hold upon Angela. They would put their heads together and whisper. They giggled over jokes known only to themselves.

Harriet, feeling an intruder, gave her attention to Jackman, tolerating him for want of better company. Jackman, himself, resenting Castlebar's preoccupation with Angela, came for the drink and pretended he had an audience of three. At that time his talk was all about movements in the desert. There were rumours of vast quantities of equipment arriving at Suez and being sent to the front. Always after dark, he said. A man with a famous name, one of a family of prestidigitators, had been flown out to Cairo and was met at parties. He was quiet and pleasant, but gave nothing away. If no one else knew why he was there, Jackman knew.

'If you hear the hun's belting back to Libya as fast as his wheels'll take him, it's because this chap has fixed up a magic show.'

'What sort of magic show?'

'Ah, that would be telling. But he creates illusions. This time, it'll be millions of them.'

'And when is this going to happen?'

'All in good time, my child.'

Meanwhile the Germans were fifty miles from Alexandria, which was exactly where they had been for the last four months. There, like the luckless engineers of some too long drawn out siege, they seemed likely to remain until boredom or starvation sent them home again.

Cookson, searching for drink and company, tracked Angela down to her table at the Union and was admitted to the company.

He came intermittently at first then, thinking he had confirmed his position, began to appear nightly to the annoyance of Castlebar who whispered to Angela. Angela murmured, 'Poor old thing, I can't tell him he's not wanted.'

'Let me do it, darling.'

'Well, if you must – but be tactful.'

'Naturally, I will.'

The next night Cookson thought he could go further: he brought a friend. He knew several people in Cairo whom no one else wanted to know and one of these was a youth who had no name but Tootsie. Before the war Tootsie had come on holiday to Egypt with his widowed mother. The mother had died, her pension had died with her and Tootsie, cut off by war from the rest of the world, wandered around, looking for someone to keep him. The sight of Tootsie lurking behind Cookson caused Castlebar to lower his eye-tooth. He made a noise in his throat like the warning growl of a guard-dog about to bark.

Cookson, aware of danger, paused nervously, then made a darting sally towards the table, saying on a high, exalted note: 'Hello, Lady H! Hello, Bill! I knew you wouldn't mind poor Tootsie . . .'

Castlebar spoke: 'Go away, Cookson. Nothing for you here.'

'Go away?' Cookson appeared flabbergasted: 'Oh, Bill, how could you be such a meanie? Tootsie and I have had such a tiring day around the bars.'

'Go away, Cookson.'

'Please, Bill, don't be horrid!' Cookson, near tears, took out his handkerchief and rolled it between his hands while Tootsie, unaware of the contention, made himself agreeable to Harriet. He had a favourite, and, indeed, an only interest in life: the state of his bowels.

He bent over Harriet to tell her: 'It's been such a week! Senna pods every night and nothing in the morning. But *nothing*! Then, only an hour ago, what a surprise! The whole bowel emptied out, and not before time, I can tell you . . .'

Harriet, who had heard about Tootsie's bowels before, held up a hand to check him while she watched Cookson, now pressing the handkerchief to his cheek, shifting from one foot to the other in shame. Tootsie, taking no notice of Harriet's appeal, continued in a small, breathy voice, asking her whether she thought the recent evacuation would be a daily event.

She shook her head and Cookson, driven beyond bearing, called to Angela: 'Dear Lady Hooper, please . . .'

Angela, who had sat with eyes lowered, was forced to look up. She said 'I'm sorry, Major Cookson. You heard what Bill said.'

'But do *you* want me to go, Lady Hooper?'

'I want what Bill wants.'

Cookson, crestfallen, plucked at Tootsie, saying, 'I understand. Come along, Tootsie. We have to go.'

As they went in confusion, Angela said with mock severity to Castlebar, 'You weren't very tactful, were you? You dreadful, lovely brute!' and she gave him an admiring kiss on the side of his mouth.

This incident had been observed by some thirty Union members, among them an oil agent called Clifford who had been one of the intruders present when Angela brought home her dead child. As Clifford keenly watched and heard Cookson's dismissal, Harriet remembered how he had recounted the story of the boy's death to the first people he met.

She was not surprised when Dobson complained to her a day or two later: 'Angela's outrageous. The whole of Cairo's talking about her wretched liaison. It's getting the flat a bad name. And where, oh where, will it all end?'

6

In the third week of October, the junior officers, NCOs and men were briefed for battle. Calling his three liaison officers together, Major Fitzwilliams addressed them in his flat, pleasant voice: 'We've all known the party was due to begin. It was just a question of how soon; and with the moon already waning, it had to be damned soon. Well, no need to tell you, it's any day now. Not tomorrow. I'd say the day after. You may feel this is short notice, but that's how Monty wants it. So, keep your traps shut, even among yourselves. There'll be plenty for you to do at the off. Meanwhile, chaps, carry on.'

Blair remained sunk into silence during the next two days and Donaldson bustled about as though preparing for action. Simon, when he sat with Blair, did not attempt to break into his abstraction. In their different ways, they suffered the tension of waiting. Simon had once led a platoon into action and experienced again the accumulating apprehension of the event ahead. But this time he did not expect to face danger, and could allow himself a self-indulgent excitement.

On the second day, they saw the reconnaissance parties going out at twilight and Blair whispered to Simon: 'This is it. Their job is to mark the starting point with tape. Then there'll be the barrage. Then the infantry go in – poor fuckers!'

'Don't the sappers go first?'

'No. The sappers clear the lanes for the tanks but the infantry have to take their chance.'

The camp emptied as the different units moved forward. There was nothing for the liaison officers at that time and they stood by the command truck like stage hands waiting for the show to commence. Donaldson, having no opportunity to flaunt his superiority, walked backwards and forwards, occasionally pausing to kick at the sand with one heel. Fitzwilliams had given each of them a copy of Montgomery's message to his troops. Simon, reading by the light of a torch, was moved by the com, mander's invocation to 'the Lord mighty in battle' and said fervently: 'Wish I was out there with them.'

Donaldson gave a guffaw of contempt: 'Don't you know the infantry went forward at daybreak? Been stuck in the slitties all day. Had to keep their heads down, too; couldn't even come up for a piss. How'd you like that? Bet you'd soon be pretty sick. What do you think, Blair?' Blair made no reply to Donaldson's perky show of knowledge but stared before him with a distracted expression as though stupefied by the onset of action.

At 19.00 hours there had been a special treat for officers and men; a hot meal of beef and carrots. Blair had not touched it and when Simon urged him to eat up, he shook his head, 'Don't fancy it, somehow.'

The moon, the great white Egyptian moon, rising above the horizon, was sharpening every object into sections of silver or black. According to rumour the attack would start at 21.00 hours but 21.00 hours came and went and there was nothing but an expectant silence. The men that remained in the camp had gathered about the command truck, all facing westwards like sightseers awaiting a firework display.

As the brilliance increased, Simon began to feel a fearful impatience, certain that the moon would reveal to the enemy the great concourse of guns and tanks moving towards the tapes. But the night, a windless and quiet night, remained still and, imagining the Germans asleep, he pitied their unsuspecting repose.

Donaldson, making approaches to his seniors, kept looking at his watch and saying knowingly: 'It'll be 22.00 hours, you see if it isn't,' but he was wrong. The barrage started twenty minutes before this predicted time.

It opened with so deafening a roar that some of the men round the truck, a mile or more from the guns, stepped back in trepidation. The timing had been perfect. Every gun had fired on the instant.

Donaldson giggled: 'Enough to make you wet your pants. What've they *got* out there, for God's sake?'

No one else spoke. The noise, a supreme awfulness of noise, went on. There was no increase of volume because there could be no increase: the pitch was at its height from the start. It shocked the nerves and its effect was made more awesome by the gun-flashes that stabbed on the horizon, orange and red, an unceasing frenzy of lights.

Simon turned to Blair and found he was no longer beside him. He was leaning against the side of the truck, hands over ears, shoulders raised as though he were being beaten about the head. Simon went to him: 'You all right, Blair?'

Blair did not reply. Simon, putting a hand on his shoulder, felt the man's body shaking and left him, unwilling to be a witness to such terror.

For fifteen minutes the uproar continued without a pause, then ended as abruptly as it had begun. The sudden silence was as unnerving as the noise, then came a sense of release. The men began excitedly to discuss what might happen next but in a moment the guns started up again.

Simon looked at Blair and saw that under this renewed onslaught, he had sunk down and was now kneeling, head against a truck wheel, about to collapse altogether. One of Fitzwilliam's messengers was bending over him and, realising his condition, returned to the office. The man reappeared a minute or two later and called Simon in.

Fitzwilliams said: 'I've a job for you, Boulderstone. I would have sent Blair but seems he's under the weather. Tanks are due to move in at 02.00 hours when the sappers have cleared the lanes. I want you to take a signal to CO, Engineers. You'll have to negotiate the mine field but they'll have gone over the near section by now. No great danger.' He looked at Simon and as though struck by his youth and inexperience, added: 'Sorry it had to be

73

you. Don't take unnecessary risks. Want you back here in one piece, old chap.'

The 'old chap' produced in Simon a choking sense of gratitude. The chance to go forward was enough. He needed no apology. He said, 'Don't worry about me, sir,' and turning, he made for the jeep at a run.

Crosbie, at the wheel, was awake simply because no living creature could sleep through the din. Yawning, he asked, 'Where are we going, sir?'

Simon scarcely knew himself but said, 'We're to take "boat" track and hope for the best.'

The tracks, each leading to a different sector of the line, were marked by symbols cut into petrol cans and lit from inside. That night there were six tracks: boat, bottle, boot and sun, moon, star. When they came on the first rough portrayal of a boat, Simon shouted, 'Get a move on, Crosbie. It'll be a piece of cake.'

Crosbie, not impressed, grunted and pressed down on the accelerator. The noise of the barrage, together with the incessant flights of aircraft going in to the attack, created a sort of blanket round the jeep so that Simon, his senses muffled, imagined they were protected by a cover no enemy shell could penetrate.

For the first half mile the going was easy; then they were caught in a dust cloud that choked them and blotted out the 'Boat' signs. Not knowing whether they were on the track or off it, Crosbie dropped his pace to a crawl, peering ahead through dust and smoke until he glimpsed the rear of a stationary vehicle. He braked, jerking them violently forward, and Simon stood up to shout: 'Hi! Where are we? We're supposed to be on "Boat" track.'

A voice bawled back: 'You try and find it, chum.'

Telling Crosbie to stay where he was, Simon jumped down and made a cautious way forward by the light of a torch. The light fell on the sand-blurred outlines of two lorries that had skidded off the track and tangled together. Other vehicles, trying to drive round them, were bogged down in soft sand. As he made his way forward, Simon began to smell the acrid smoke of bursting shells. The shells threw up immense fountains of sand that showered down on men and trucks. Realising he was not, after all, immune from danger, Simon went back for his tin hat. Starting out again, he saw ahead of him a point of light that grew into a blaze. He was almost upon it before he could see that a truck had caught fire. Enemy mortars were bursting over it while the crew was trying to douse the flames with water from a supply tank. As he stopped, struck by the infernal confusion of the scene, an officer shouted to him: 'Get out of the way, you jackass. She's loaded with ammunition.'

'I must get through. I've a signal for CO, Engineers on "Boat" track.'

"Then get past, quick as your feet will carry you. Keep your head down. If you see a trip wire, give it a wide berth or you'll get your bollocks blown off.'

Taking this as a joke, Simon asked, 'How far do the mine fields stretch?'

'How the hell do I know. Probably twenty miles.'

Eyes streaming, throat raw with smoke, Simon sped round the ammunition truck, making for the noise of the guns. As their shapes appeared through the fog, he began to stumble on what seemed a stony beach. Lowering his torch, he saw the mardam was thickly covered with shrapnel fragments, jagged, blue-grey and crystalline from the super-heat of explosion. This shrapnel carpet stretched between the guns and many yards beyond them. There was no question of running over it and he picked his way as best he could until he was out in the open area of no-man's-land. The fog still hung in the air and even the moon was lost to sight. The mine fields were here. He expected to find the sappers somewhere ahead, but instead of the sappers, he came upon a pride of tanks, just visible, monstrous through the smoky dust. Grinding and rumbling, they were edging forward so slowly, he could pass them at a walk. The heat of the armour came out to him and he could smell, above the fumes of the explosive, the stench of exhausts.

Stumbling in the dark, he all but fell in the path of one of them and someone shouted from above, 'What d'you think you're doing down there?'

The tank commander was not much older than Simon and, bending down, his harassed young face lightened as Simon looked up. Seeing another like himself riding into battle, Simon could have cried in envy but all he said was, 'Sorry. I'm liaison. Had to leave my jeep behind and go it on foot. I'm trying to find CO, Sappers.'

'He'll be up front, where you might expect. And if you want to make it, keep clear of our treads. At the rate we're going, it'd be a slow and sticky finish.'

The rows of widely spaced tanks seemed endless but at last, dodging among them, almost blinded by the sand they threw up, Simon was suddenly out in clear air with the moon, tranquil and uninvolved, high above him. In the distance two searchlights, shifting in the sky, crossed and remained crossed, at a point a few miles forward. Someone had told him that their intersection would mark the objective of the advance and he stopped for a moment to marvel at the sight. Then he started to run with long strides, enjoying his freedom from vehicles and smoke, supposing the sappers were at hand. For a brief period he could see the western horizon agitated by flashes from the anti-tank guns then the dust clouded the air again and he realised there were men ahead of him, shadows, noiseless because their noise was lost in the greater noise of exploding shells, a field of ghosts. He had gone too far. He had reached the rear of the advancing infantry.

Walking two or three yards apart, their rifles held at the high port, bayonets fixed, the men went at a sort of crawling trudge under the shower of shells and mortars. They were on the mine fields, watching for trip wires. Each man had a pack between his shoulder blades and each pack was painted with a white cross, a marker for the man behind.

As Simon paused, uncertain what to do next, a man fell nearby and he went to him with some thought of giving help. The man, a thin, undersized youth, lay on his back and as the eyes gazed blankly at him, Simon was reminded of the death of Arnold and he wanted to take the body out of danger. Then he realised he was behaving like a fool. His job was to deliver a signal, not to get himself killed.

Having crossed the near section of the mine fields without a sight of the sappers, he was at a loss: where should he go, left or right? He ran to one of the slow, forward-pacing men and seized hold of his arm. The man, encapsulated in his own anxiety, gave a cry then stared at Simon in astonishment. Bending close to him, Simon shouted 'I've a signal for CO, Engineers. Where can I find them?'

The man twisted away as though from a lunatic and Simon let him go, then, running across the tide of the advance, came out into moonlight that whitened vast stretches of empty sand. The barrage had stopped again and despite the distant thud of guns, the effect was of silence through which he heard from somewhere far away the high whine of bagpipes. The music, as fragmentary as the singing of 'Lili Marlene', gradually faded out and he remembered there was no Scottish regiment in his corps. He knew he was lost. Having gone so eagerly into the fight, he now only wanted to get back to base.

He waited till the barrage renewed itself then, guided by the gun flashes, he ran towards the gun emplacements and came upon a group of men working intently together, lit by the star bursts of enemy shells. There were three men, one of them holding a long tube to which was fitted a plate, like a bed-warmer, which he slid over the sand surface. His companions watched with the tense attention of men to whom death was an immediate possibility. Simon stopped and stared at the mine-detector plate, fearful of interrupting the search. The man paused. He had found something. The second man marked the spot with tape and the third pinned the tape to the ground; then the three knelt and felt out the shape in the sand with questing fingers, as delicate as surgeons palpating an abdomen. Simon remained where he was till the mine was lifted, immobilised and put on one side, then he said, 'Sir!' They looked up, aware of his presence for the first time.

'I'm liaison. I've a signal for CO, Engineers.'

Without speaking, one of the three pointed to another group of men that stood darkly in the distance, then returned to the search.

The CO, receiving the signal, said, 'Have any difficulty finding us?'

'No, sir.'

'Clever lad. Report back "Detectors working OK".'

Triumphant, Simon put his head down and ran towards the barrage. Stumbling through the shrapnel fragments, he passed between the gun emplacements and found a supply truck starting back to the depot. Shouting to it to stop, he was taken back to his jeep that stood where he had left it, with Crosbie asleep over the wheel.

Crosbie, wakened, started at the sight of Simon's smoke blackened face and said, 'Where you been, sir?'

'Where d'you think? Delivering the signal, of course.'

'What's it like out there?'

'Not too good. Come on, Crosbie, let's get back.'

Expecting to be congratulated, Simon was disappointed when his safe return had so little effect on Fitzwilliams who said, 'All right, Boulderstone, get some sleep if you can. I've had to send Blair to the MO, so you and Donaldson will have to do a bit more.'

'Sorry about Blair, sir. Hope it's nothing serious?'

'I don't know. Could be that infectious jaundice. Lot of it around.' Having spoken, Fitzwilliams stuck out his lower lip so it was evident he knew exactly what was wrong with Blair.

Getting into his sleeping-bag, too tired to notice the noise of the barrage, Simon looked at his watch and saw it was four a.m., the latest he had ever been up in his life. He thought of the ghostly men, each with a white cross on his back, and imagined them still moving through the night. He almost envied them but greater than envy was his desire for sleep.

He was roused two hours later by Crosbie who handed him a mug of tea. Crosbie, wakened by the camp guard, said, 'We've got to go out again, sir. You're wanted at the command truck.'

Pulling on his jersey and gulping his tea, Simon went to the truck where a young captain called Dawson had taken over from Fitzwilliams. Simon, newly awake, was slightly unsteady and Dawson eyed him severely: 'Anything the matter?'

'No, sir. Didn't get much sleep, sir, that's all.'

'Most of our chaps'll get no sleep at all tonight. Now, we've had a signal from Corps CO. One of our armoured divisions has failed to reach its objective and the radio's haywire. No joy on the inter-com, either. So, there's nothing for it. You'll have to go and find what's holding them up.'

'Sir. Any idea where they are, sir?'

'Um!' Dawson said musingly: 'Thought you might ask that.' He straightened out a hand-drawn map of the positions, or supposed positions, of the different units and examined it with his head in his hands: 'Um, um, um! They're supposed to be in the northern corridor on their way to the final objective. That doesn't tell you much, does it?'

'What *is* the final objective, sir?'

'Up here it's Kidney Ridge, down there it's the Miteiriya. Ever heard of the Miteiriya?'

'Yes, sir.' It was fire from the Miteiriya Ridge that had killed Hugo and all the members of his patrol. But Hugo's death now seemed far in the past. Having seen what he had seen, Simon knew that if his brother had not died that time, he would, as likely as not, have died in the present battle.

Looking at Dawson's map, Simon saw the two broad arrows aimed, the one at Kidney Ridge, the other at the Miteiriya, and thought how simple and ordered the advance appeared on paper and what blinding confusion it was in fact.

'Which route shall I take, sir?'

'Find one that aims at the northern corridor. The corridor was supposed to be clear by daylight and the division on its way through. Ideally, they'd be out in the open by now, but they're not. Either they're off route and fart-arsing around, or they've been shot up by fire from Tel el Eisa. Either way, they're stuck. Your job is to contact Corps Commander and ask him what the hell? Or, in official language: "Is his division properly set up for the attack?" Got it? Any questions?'

'No, sir, no questions.'

The sun was now above the horizon. The barrage had ended at daybreak and with the main guns silent, the lesser guns – tank,

79

machine, anti-aircraft – merged into a screen of noise so continuous the ear ceased to notice it. Seeing the dust of battle blotting out the western horizon, Simon no longer felt an eagerness for the fight. He knew what lay ahead and was reluctant to return to it. Yet he was luckier than most: he had had two hours sleep while other men, as Dawson had reminded him, had spent the night in danger and wakefulness.

They met the dust cloud where it had been the night before. Ambulances, appearing from it, were taking the severely wounded to the field hospital behind the camp. A mile further on, the jeep passed the dressing-station where men, awaiting transport, lay on stretchers on the ground itself, or sat, some alert, some with head down on knees, maimed, bloody and exhausted.

All the flies of the desert seemed to have been drawn here by the smell of festering flesh. Simon urged Crosbie to 'step on it' but there was worse to come. Less than a hundred yards further on, a mass grave had been dug to receive the dead. It was not yet full. A sickly effluvium came from it and flies hung over it like a shroud of black. Crosbie swerved, attempting to avoid its malodour, and ran off the track. The jeep ploughed into soft sand. It stopped and they were at once set upon by swarms of flies, some no bigger than gnats, attacking the eyes and lips of the two men who, unable to escape, set to digging and putting mats under the wheels.

Eventually, jerking the jeep back to the track, they ran onto an empty track where Simon feared they might have driven beyond the battle area. Then two vehicles appeared on the road ahead. Distorted by the first wavering of mirage, they were difficult to identify but, seeing they were stationary, Simon told Crosbie to draw up. Walking towards them, he was disconcerted to see they were staff cars and four angry senior officers were arguing in front of them. As he approached, one of them was shouting, 'I still say it's not the way to use tanks,' and Simon hoped the tanks in question were the ones he was seeking. The four officers had an appearance of unnerving importance but one of them had noticed Simon and he felt it would be cowardly to retreat. He said, 'Excuse me, sir,' and as he spoke, all the men swung round on him in exasperated enquiry. He explained his mission and the one who had first noticed him, waved him on: 'They're about a mile up the track.'

'Are they out of the mine field, sir?'

'No, they're not out of the mine field – and if you want to know why, I suggest you toddle along and ask them.'

As Simon climbed back into the jeep, Crosbie muttered, 'Ratty bastard,' and Simon saw no reason to reprimand him.

From the churned up sand, the overturned markers, the smell of burnt oil and the thickening dust, it was soon evident that they were in the wake of an armoured division. They were also within range of enemy fire. Breathing in sand particles and the astringent smoke from mortars and shells, they bumped forward, swaying in ruts and tilting over sandhills, and passing vehicles that had been disabled and abandoned. A dispatch rider came out of the dust; Simon shouted, 'How far ahead are they?'

The rider stopped and leaning back over his dispatch box, pointed to a black cloud on the horizon: 'That's them. You'll catch them up in no time: they're down to a crawl.'

But nearly an hour passed before Simon came in sight of the rear tanks, a line spaced over so wide a field the flanking vehicles were almost out of sight. The blanket of smoke about them was like the blanket of night. The tanks appeared to be motionless but coming close behind them, Simon saw they were making a very slight headway into a fog that was peppered with the star flash of bursting shells.

Crosbie braked, and turned uncertainly to Simon. He did not try to speak but his expression asked: 'Must we go into this?'

Standing up, Simon could see that one of the nearer tanks had come to a stop and the bailed-out crew was starting to dig in. He motioned Crosbie to drive towards it but as the jeep turned, shells fell about them and Crosbie stopped again. Trying to keep up his own courage, Simon bawled at him, 'Get a move on, Crosbie!' and they continued with flak hitting their tin hats and striking the sides of the jeep. At the sight of them, the tank commander waved them furiously away: 'What the hell are you doing here? Go back. You're drawing enemy fire.'

Awaiting no further encouragement, Crosbie swung the jeep round and tried to fly the field but Simon, catching hold of the wheel, forced him to stop.

Simon knew he must again make his way forward on foot. Ordering Crosbie to drive back to the track and wait, he ran to the tank crew and asked where he could find the CO. The tank commander answered with disgruntled brevity: 'Up front. 'Bout a mile,' then as Simon started forward, shouted after him: 'And don't take that bloody jeep. Everything that moves, draws fire.'

Bent almost double, finding what cover he could from each tank as he reached it, Simon went at a good pace but slackened every few minutes to ask direction from the tank commanders. The commanders, bored and irritated by the delays, sweating in the heat generated by the slow grind forward, were as perfunctory as the first man. No one knew for sure where the CO was to be found. All they could do was gesture him towards the forward sector where the leading tanks had come to a stop. The way ahead was lit by blazing tanks, and tank crews were tramping back to dig themselves in when they found a likely space. Bren carriers, looking for wounded, came out of the dust, swaying about until they made sufficient speed to steady themselves.

At the front of the advance, which was less an advance than a standstill, enemy shelling was intense. Crouching behind tanks, darting on whenever there was an instant's respite, Simon's progress was slow. As he sheltered behind one tank, a shell burst over it, not penetrating the fabric but showering it with burning oil that spattered his shoulders. Small flames sprang up over his jersey and as he gathered up sand to quench them, the whole tank was enveloped in fire and he threw himself down, rolling on the ground until he was away from the conflagration.

He found the commanding officer sitting on the lee side of his tank in an attitude of despondent impatience. Having read the signal, the commander said in a strained voice: 'The Scorpions broke down. Fault was the flails raised too much dust, damned things over-heated and the sappers had to scrap them. Half the detectors brought up were faulty and now the chaps are down to bayonet prodding. Slow business. That's why we're stuck here. Lot of sitting ducks.'

'You know your radio's packed up, sir?'

'Yep. We were shot up and shrapnel knocked it out. We've given it a shake but the damned thing's kaput . . .' he stopped then as though galvanised, shouted at the top of his voice: 'We're breaking through.' The tanks began to roll forward and at once, as though the movement had been a sign to heaven, the sinking sun cut the fog with a shaft of orange light and enemy fire became furious. The CO ordered Simon away: 'Ruddy counter-attack just as we've got the light in our eyes. Better dig in till the show's over. Goodbye. Good luck.'

Making his way back between the advancing tanks, Simon came on a trench and threw himself into it. The men in possession gave him space and they all sat together, speechless beneath the uproar of battle. Too tired now to care what was going on, Simon sank into drowsiness, imagining himself back in Garden City with Edwina, in her long, white dress, smiling her conciliatory smile. Now he did not feel resentment but a confused pity for her and for all womankind. In a world where men died young, what was a girl to do? Facing life alone, she had to fend for herself. He murmured, 'Poor little thing! Poor little thing!' then sleep came down on him.

He woke at daybreak to find himself alone in the trench. The noises of the night had come to a stop and, climbing out, he found the tanks had advanced out of sight. He had the field to himself – but not quite to himself. Burnt out tanks stood about him like disabled crows and the smell of burning was heavy on the air. There were dead men and men not yet dead, and the Brens were returning to pick them up.

As the sun topped the horizon, the first, subtle light of day swept like a wave over the desert and about him, and passed on, lighting desert and more desert, miles of desert that had once been no-man's-land. He was not sure now whether the division's objective had been Kidney Ridge or the Miteiriya but it was in no-man's-land that Hugo had died. He had bled to death like the dead left behind by the battle and perhaps he had lain here, on this barren ground that was now the field of victory.

Walking back among tanks as useless as the sand they stood on, stepping over the bodies of lost young men, Simon asked, 'Is this what Hugo died for? And am I to die for this?' There was no one to answer him and as he realised how hungry he was, he forgot his own questions and started to run.

7

Castlebar who, once a week, went to tutor a Greek boy in Alexandria, came back with the news that there was heavy combat in the desert. It vibrated through roads and pavements and at times, when the air was very still, people could hear the boom of guns. No news had been released. No one knew what was happening but Castlebar was sure that this was a major battle.

Jackman, not too pleased that Castlebar should be the bringer of such tidings, said, 'Of course it is. Didn't I tell you something was on? What do you think the preparations have been for? This is it.'

Still, there was no certainty. Alex, like Cairo, was a city of rumours. The gunfire might mean a German offensive or merely a minor skirmish, or the Afrika Korps sending a parthian shot before packing and leaving their long-held position. Ten days passed then the civilians were allowed to know that there had been a second battle of Alamein, the greatest battle of the desert war. The allied forces were pushing Rommel back to the frontier and perhaps even further than that.

Meanwhile, an extraordinary thing happened. The sun, the great god of Egypt, disappeared and the noonday sky, so constant in its brilliance, was hidden behind cloud. A biblical darkness overhung the city and people, hastening in the streets, feared a cataclysm – the day of judgement or, at the least, an earthquake – and sought what cover they could find.

Angela and Harriet were out at the time. Harriet, finding that

Angela hardly knew where the Muski was, insisted they must go there. She said, 'You should learn how the other half live,' and she led her through the narrow, dusky lanes to her favourite shop: a twilit place, like a vast tent, where old glass and china orna‑ments were heaped together on shelves and floor. In the centre of this disordered treasure store, there was a glass case lit by acetylene lamps and full of gleaming jewels. Harriet called Angela to it: 'Come and see the rose‑diamonds.'

The rose‑diamonds, set in pinkish gold, were formed into brooches, earrings, bracelets and necklaces, and Harriet, who could not afford to buy them, was attracted by their elaborate opulence. Angela, lifting the pieces and examining them, asked, 'What are rose‑diamonds? They look like sugar crystals.'

Harriet repeated the question to a man in a dirty galabiah who stood guard over the case. He replied in an aloof manner, having superior knowledge: 'Rosy di'mints? – they is di'mints.'

Angela laughed, 'So now we know. Shall I buy one for Bill?' She picked among the designs, rejecting the flowers, and came upon a brooch in the shape of a heart: 'What about this? I'll give it to him for a giggle.' She did not haggle over the price but, paying what the shop‑keeper asked, she laughed excitedly at the thought of giving the large, diamond‑studded heart to Castlebar.

Coming out of the shop, they found the outdoors nearly as dark as the indoors. Made nervous by the unusual gloom, they hurried through the lanes, instinctively making for the European quarter as though there they might escape the ominous sky. But in the Esbekiyah the sky grew more ominous. The office workers were coming out for the siesta and the businessmen who could afford taxis were squabbling over them. As the first rain fell, one man covered his fez with his pocket‑handkerchief and before the pavements were wet, every fez was protected by a covering of some sort. Drops, heavy and immense, splashed down and merged into each other, and the Egyptians began to panic at the sight. The two women, having reached the western end of the Esbekiyah, ran to Shepeard's Hotel and there, standing under the canopy, they watched the gutters flow and overflow, then cover the streets. Cairo had no main drainage and the water, speeding like a river past the hotel, could only flow down the Kasr el Nil until it lost itself in the Nile.

The shop owners, opposite the hotel, were wading up to their knees, putting up shutters as though against a riot. Cars, forced to a stop, stood in the stream with passengers waving and begging for rescue, though there was no one to rescue them.

One of the men gathered under the canopy, said, 'They will be drown'ed' and this possibility was discussed around Harriet and Angela with sombre satisfaction. Angela said, 'It's too heavy to last,' but it did last and, becoming bored with it, she suggested they go inside and have a drink.

Staff officers, who regarded the place as their own, filled every chair in the main rooms and possessed every table. When they showed no sign of moving, Angela said loudly, with a gleeful contempt, 'When I was a little girl, during the First War, I heard the term "temporary gentleman". I couldn't think what it meant then, but now I know.' At this, two of the officers rose and Angela, saying, 'Oh, too kind!', smiled upon them and sat down.

Delighted by her success, she laughed and winked at Harriet, but this mood did not last. The latest communiqué from the front stated 'Axis forces in full retreat'. This news, that had rejoiced the British in Cairo, had merely perturbed Angela.

She said to Harriet: 'I don't like it. If the army leaves here, that bitch will stand a much better chance of getting back.'

'What do you think would happen if she got back?'

'Bill says he intends telling her he's finished with her.'

Pondering on the fact that both her friends were enamoured of men whom they might never have for their own, Harriet could see that uncertainty was a strong potion and said: 'Angela, would you want Castlebar so much if he didn't belong to someone else?'

Angela put the question aside with a gesture: 'Don't let's think any more about it.' Looking into her bag, she brought out the rose-diamond brooch to distract them: ' "Rosy di'mints? They is di'mints." Wasn't that wonderful? Come on, let's go to the restaurant and eat.'

The noise of the rain stopped while they were at luncheon but when they returned to the terrace, they found they were trapped by the stream that still filled the street and held captive the occupants of the cars. Another hour passed before the last of it, a long, low ripple of water, slid down Kasr el Nil and away. The sun broke through the clouds, the roads began to steam, dry circular patches appeared on the paving stones, drivers struggled to restart their engines, and Harriet and Angela were released.

But that was not all. The rain had watered not only the city but the surrounding desert with remarkable consequences. The papers reported a marvel: seed that had lain for years dormant in the sand, sprang up and blossomed but the great age of the seeds prevented normal growth. The flowers were miniatures of their kind. Dobson, reading this at breakfast, said he had heard that the Saccara sands were covered with flowers.

'A garden,' he said, 'a veritable garden!' and Harriet, turning eagerly to Guy, put her hand on his arm: 'It's your free day. Do let us go and see it.'

'How would we get there?' The tram-line ended at Mena House.

'But why can't we take a taxi?'

Guy laughed at the idea of taking a taxi into the desert: 'I've better things to do,' he said and Harriet knew he had meant to refuse from the start.

'But it's your free day.'

'That's when I really work. I'm preparing my troops' enter-tainment. I've a hundred and one things to do.'

Guy had begun to plan the entertainment some time before and Harriet had hoped that by now it was forgotten. But it was not forgotten. 'Haven't the troops enough entertainments?'

'This will be no ordinary show.' To prevent further argument, he jumped up, his breakfast unfinished, as Hassan was putting down a bowl of fruit steeped in permanganate. He took a couple of guavas, splashing the cloth with purple fluid, and called out as he went: 'Sorry about that.'

Dobson looked after him: 'What energy! What a man! He never stops, does he?'

'No, never. How would you like to be married to him?'

'Oh, come now, Harriet. You wouldn't have him any different?'

'Wouldn't I? These entertainments worry me to death. Suppose this one fails?'

'Not likely. He's got ENSA backing.'

Harriet said, 'How do you know?': then, too late, realised she was admitting her own ignorance and put in a second question to erase the first: 'Why should ENSA back Guy's show?'

'You know what he's like! He could charm the monkeys down from the trees.'

'Yes.' Harriet sat silent for a few minutes then said, 'I wish I were a man fighting in the desert.'

'You'd find it a very great bore.'

'It couldn't be worse than our life here.'

'Here? Most Englishwomen think they're damned lucky to be here.'

'Well, I'm not most Englishwomen.'

Edwina was supposed to be on duty at the Embassy but, coming slowly to the table, her hand to her brow, her hair dishevelled, she said in a small voice: 'Oh, Dobbie, I've got such a head. I don't think I can go in this morning.'

Dobson, in a tone of bantering commiseration, said, 'Poor thing! Then I suppose we'll have to manage without you. What about the evening stint?'

'I'll try, Dobbie dear.'

Dobson left for the Embassy and Edwina drooped over the table, sighing, until the telephone rang. Coming to instant life, she reached it before Hassan had found his way into the hall. Harriet, hearing one side of an animated conversation, gathered that Peter Lisdoonvarna had the morning off and was taking Edwina out. She came back to say, 'Oh, Harriet, to think I might have been at the office. What luck I was here!' She danced away crying, 'What luck! What luck! What luck!'

Harriet, hearing her singing as she splashed under the shower, envied her excitement. That, Harriet thought, was what women most wanted, and what risks they took to attain it. She, herself, had married and travelled to the other side of Europe with some⁄

one she barely knew. She might have been abandoned there. She might have been murdered. In fact, she had suffered no more than disappointment, finding that her husband's devotion to all comers left little room for her.

She was still sitting over her coffee when Peter Lisdoonvarna arrived, giving off vigour like a magnetic force. The shutters had been closed but the semi-darkness seemed to disperse itself as he gave Harriet a hearty kiss on the lips. All good-looking girls were Peter's girls and he approached them with such boisterous confidence, few could resist him. Edwina shouted to him from her room but he was quite happy to stay with Harriet, telling her he had just bought King Farouk's second-best Bentley.

'Magnificent job! Been angling for it for weeks. Park Ward body. Eight-litre chassis. Bonnet as long as the gun on a Panzer Mark III. I know some chaps don't think it's worth owning a car out here, but I'm the car-owning type. Like to know it's there. Get in and push off, no hanging around for taxis. You've got to have some relaxation after the stultifying, bloody chores at HQ. Care for a spin? Like to try her out?'

Harriet felt there was nothing she would like better, but what of Edwina? Hesitating, she asked, 'Where are you going?'

'Don't know. Haven't thought about it. Anywhere you like.'

'Would you go to Saccara?'

'Why not? Saccara it is!' As Edwina came into the room, he shouted: 'Come on, then, girls.'

Edwina hesitated only a moment before she smiled and said, 'Is Harriet coming with us? How lovely!'

The car, standing outside the house, was indeed magnificent. Harriet was put into the spacious back seat and when they were under way, was soon forgotten. Edwina, having spent her enthusiasm about the car, put an arm round Peter's shoulder and her head against his head, but Peter still gave his attention to the Bentley's splendour. 'All leather upholstery,' he said.

'Leather, really?' Edwina spoke as though leather were an unheard of luxury.

Peter demonstrated the automatic opening and closing of the windows, and the button that sent the canvas roof folding back behind the seats. Harriet attempted to murmur her appreciation but anything she said was lost behind Edwina's gasps and squeals of wonder.

Unable to compete, Harriet looked out of her side window to see what could be seen. And she saw a peasant, head bound up in a scarf, mooning along the pavement. The scarf indicated that he had toothache or a cold, but she knew he was not thinking of his ailments. Instead he was telling himself one of the fantasies that compensated the poor for their poverty. A shop-keeper had once told her that a rich American lady had fallen in love with a guide at the pyramids and gone to live with him in his one-roomed village hut. Harriet had laughed at the story but the shop-keeper believed it because belief made life tolerable. She knew the peasant in the scarf, grinning, head wagging, was imagining just such a romance for himself.

Out on the Saccara road, Peter said, 'Like to travel at m'own speed,' and pressing on the accelerator, the car sped through villages, scattering children and chickens and causing the villagers to shout after him in rage. Someone must have telephoned the sugar factory at El-Hawandiyen for the factory workers had gathered outside the building with stones in their hands. The hood was down and seeing women in the car, most of them let the stones fall harmlessly but two let fly and hit the side of the car. Edwina screamed, hiding her face in Peter's shoulder, and he replaced the hood and latched it. He did this without losing speed while he grumbled: 'Damned fool country, this is! Can't take a gallop without chaps chucking stones. Wish I was back in the blue. Do what you like there.'

Edwina, folded against Peter, murmured: 'Oh, Peter, you know you don't want to leave me!'

'Perhaps not, but I'm a soldier, not a ruddy pen-pusher.'

They reached the hummocked site that had once been the great city of Memphis. Colossal statues lay among the palm groves but these held no interest for Peter who drove on rapidly, seeing no cause to stop until the track ended at Mariette's house.

It was mid-day when, even in winter, the temperature was high. Rubbing the sweat from his broad nose, Peter said, 'Let's get under cover,' and pulling Edwina with him, he made for the Serapeum, the enclosure of the sacred bulls.

Harriet, walking round, looked for the miniature flowers but they had scarcely had time to open before the sun sucked up their moisture and now nothing remained but dry stalks, like matchsticks stuck in the sand. But there were other tokens of the rain. Fragments of fallen temples had been washed to the surface and she came on a stone lotus, half of which had been buried until now. The exposed half was pitted by time but the other, newly revealed, was as smooth as flesh. The wet wind had set the surface into long, sculpted folds, washed to a salty whiteness, and Harriet felt well rewarded for her journey in the back seat.

When she first went into the Serapeum, she could see no sign of Peter and Edwina, but then she came on them, obscure in the shadows, their bodies pressed together as though each sought to merge into the other. Hearing her, they parted for an instant then at once rejoined and she moved away, feeling the solitude of those who are outside the circle of ecstasy. She wandered to the other end of the gallery and waited till the others tired of their dalliance. Edwina, giving a scream, broke away from Peter and he pursued her round the huge sarcophagi then, seizing her, he pushed her down onto a slab of black granite and threw himself on top of her. She cried out, almost smothered by his weight: 'Peter, oh Peter, you're killing me.' He let her go and she sprang up, laughing provocatively, and the pursuit began again.

Harriet, turning her back on them as they embraced, reflected that this burial place of bulls, that had become lords of the western world, might well inspire Peter who was a bull himself and a lord, though of a different kind. She did not know whether the frenzy had a climax but she heard Peter say, finality in his voice: 'All right, let's go. We'll trundle back to Mena for lunch.'

They had not seen much but it did not occur to Peter that there was anything to see. As for luncheon, he took it for granted that Mena would please the women and he was right. Edwina smiled on Harriet as though she were bestowing a gift on her and Harriet smiled back, acknowledging the benefaction.

But at the hotel, the porter told them that bar and restaurant were full and they would have to wait. Harriet suggested they go and look at the matrix of the Ship of the Sun, the ship that daily crossed the heavens and at night sank down into the underworld.

Peter laughed, 'I've had enough of the bloody sun. I'm going to powder m'nose,' and left the women to go alone and look down into the concave cradle which had once held the sacred ship.

When they entered the hotel vestibule, Peter was standing with three other officers, his brows drawn blackly together. Edwina whispered, 'What do you think they're telling him?' but both women knew that the talk could only be about the desert conflict.

He was still frowning when he joined them and Edwina, trying to catch hold of his hand, asked, 'What's the matter, darling?'

Avoiding her grasp, he said, 'I'm missing the whole damned shooting match. That's all. Let's go and eat.'

Luncheon, which was to have been a pleasure, was no pleasure at all. Peter, silent in discontent, ignored Edwina who stared helplessly at him then turned to Harriet with an expression that said, 'See what I have to put up with!' Harriet, no longer excluded by their love-making, now felt an intruder upon a situation which she could do nothing to help.

Driving back between the bean fields into the Cairo suburbs, Edwina whispered, 'Honestly, Teddy-bear, do you really want to go back to the desert?'

'Yep.'

'But what would poor Edwina do without her Teddy-bear?'

'Find another Teddy-bear.'

'I only want you.'

The sweet scent of the bean fields filled the air but it meant nothing to Edwina who, in anguish, moved from one desperate manoeuvre to another. In a wheedling whisper she said: 'If we were married, or even engaged, it would not be so bad.'

'Why? What difference would that make?'

'All the difference in the world. We'd belong. I'd have a right to know if anything happened to you.'

'The old next-of-kin, eh?' Peter gave an ironical chuckle.

'Darling, I'm serious.'

'Don't be serious, old girl. I'm not worth it. Not good enough for you . . .'

Could there, Harriet wondered, be a more discouraging rejection than that? But Edwina refused to be discouraged. She protested that Peter was all she wanted. Half weeping, she pleaded her love for him while he stared at the road as though hearing nothing. At last, as her voice dissolved in tears, he said: 'Look here, old thing. The truth is, I'm all tied up.'

'You . . . you mean you're engaged?'

'Something like that.' He gave a laugh and Edwina thought he might be teasing.

'Who bothers about engagements these days? The war could go on for years. I bet, by the time you get back, she'll have married someone else.' When Peter laughed again, Edwina persisted: 'Perhaps she *has* married someone else already.'

'Not very likely.'

'You're pulling my leg, aren't you?'

'Who could resist it?' he patted her knee: 'Such a nice, long leg!'

They were crossing the river and among the noise of the Bulaq traffic Edwina let the matter drop for the moment, but she could not resist a last triumphant shot: 'Still, you can't get back to the desert, can you?'

Peter glumly agreed: 'Doesn't look like it.'

Smiling to herself, Edwina took out her compact and looked at her pretty face. The war was on her side. It kept Peter in Egypt and the authorities kept him in Cairo. He was with her and while he was with her, she had reason to hope. The conversation, that had disturbed Harriet, seemed to have had little effect on Edwina. She powdered her face and moved close to Peter again. They were reconciled and when the women left the car in Garden City, he said, 'What are you doing tonight, old girl?'

'Nothing in particular.'

'Call for you around eight, then?'

'Oh, lovely, darling. See you soon.'

She went joyfully up the steps to the flat confident, it seemed, she would win him in the end.

8

On the fourth day of battle, relays of exhausted men came into the camp to be replaced by reserve troops. These men, most of them from tanks, had been lucky to get three hours sleep in a night and Simon, when he heard this, felt ashamed of his own nervous fatigue. Unable to excuse himself, he told himself that he would have done better to remain under fire and become conditioned to it. The rest periods between his sorties into action, and the fact he was liable to be wakened at any hour of the night, had demoralised him.

He had little or no idea what had been gained by the fighting and Fitzwilliams, though he questioned the returning men, could not tell him much. The general belief was that in the northern sector British armour had driven a wedge into the German defences but no sooner had this news gone round, than the commander in the sector radioed to say that his whole brigade was ringed by enemy anti-tank guns.

Fitzwilliams, like the officers Simon had approached on the road, was critical of the strategy of the battle: 'Bad show, I call it. Suppose the brass hats know what they're doing, but I've never heard of tanks being sent into a breach. Could lose the whole damn lot.'

For a while it seemed that if not lost, the battle was petering out. There were a couple of empty days for Simon who had become used to action and felt the need for excitement. He hung around the command vehicle in a state of restless boredom; then a fresh offensive began. Given a signal to deliver, he ran gleefully to the

jeep shouting, 'Come on, Crosbie, wake up. This is the life.'
Crosbie, baffled as usual by Simon's moods, grunted and muttered, 'Sir.'

At the end of October, the division to which Simon belonged
was withdrawn from the line. The tank crews, decimated by
continuous fighting, were ordered back to reserve positions and
Simon was assigned a new sector. He had to report to a coastal
area where a fresh division was being prepared for an attack.

When he set out, November was beginning with dramatic
splendour. The sky, that had dazzled the sight with its brazen
emptiness, was filling with immense cumulous clouds. They were
rising out of the sea and stretching, as though each was trying to
over-top the other, until by mid-day they had reached the zenith.
They were of different colours: one was a dark purple, its neighbour,
swelling up behind, was azure, while on either side of them
billowing curves of wool white, catching the sun on outer rims,
gleamed like mother-of-pearl.

Simon, amazed by this display, said to Crosbie, 'What do
you make of it?'

Raising his eyes without lifting his head, Crosbie muttered,
'Looks like trouble to me.'

The dark cloud grew until it dominated the sky. The wind
strengthened in the unusual gloom and the sand lifted, but the
storm did not break until the men were in sight of the camp.
Then rain came at them like a slanting curtain, as hard and rough
as emery paper, and clattered against the jeep. The road was
blotted out. Crosbie braked and flung himself round to find
ground-sheets in the back of the jeep. They wrapped themselves
up and waited for the deluge to slacken. The rain stopped within
minutes but the camp, when they reached it, was under water.

Dawson, in the command vehicle, told Simon they were preparing to move forward. The new arrivals would be lucky if they
could find themselves tea and bully.

The men, plashing through puddles, were shifting equipment.

Though the water sank rapidly, the ground was left muddy and a wetness hung in the air. Dawson had been right about food. Crosbie, sent to forage, came back with mugs of tea and a couple of bully-beef sandwiches. They would have to spend the night in the jeep. Crosbie took up his favourite position, sprawled over the wheel and Simon climbed into the back seat. He wakened, cramped and chilly, at midnight when the petrol replenishing lorries went out. Then the barrage started up again, and turning on his back, staring up at the starless sky, he felt the war would never end. This, he told himself, could be his whole life and it might be a short life. He was as liable as any man in the field to be killed by the enemy. He turned towards the jeep back and tried to lose his old, abiding fear in sleep but just as he was drifting off, a messenger shook him and ordered him to the command vehicle.

Dawson had gone off duty and a stranger was in charge of the command truck. He sounded as disconsolate as Simon felt. "Fraid I've got to send you up front. The Kiwis are supposed to be advancing on Fuka but they've hit a snag. They say there's an unmapped mine field in their path. Well, here . . .' he spread out a hand-drawn sketch of the field; '. . . it's marked as a dummy, put down by our chaps last June. The commander won't take my word for it. Says it's too risky. Says he'll dig in till he gets further orders. You'll have to take this along to show him. Let him see for himself. Right?'

'Sir. Which route, sir?'

'God knows. All the routes are in a mess. Sheer, bloody shambles between here and Tel el Eisa. Try "Star", it's no worse than the others. If you can't find it, you'll have to ask as you go.'

Setting out, Simon had no more zest for the journey than Crosbie had. The battle had gone on too long and all he could feel now was a racking weariness.

The track, churned up by vehicles, had dried and hardened to the consistency of concrete and the jeep rocked on ridges and skidded through slime left by puddles. The sky had cleared and the waning moon gave a bleak, dispirited light.

The track was soon lost and they made their way guided by

staccato flashes on the western horizon. They had covered little more than a mile when Simon realised the division had driven straight through an enemy position. The tanks standing idle about them were German tanks; the bodies propped up in slit trenches wore German headgear and the black-clad figures that trudged past the jeep, avoiding it with blundering steps, were unarmed Germans who had given themselves up. The tank commanders, with no room or time for prisoners, had sent them back and now they were making their own way into captivity. Thankfully, Simon imagined. Once they reached the camp, they would throw themselves down to sleep and Simon wished he could do the same.

Crosbie had other thoughts. Looking askance at the burnt-out tanks, he at last reached the point of speech, 'You seen inside these ruddy Marks? God, what a sight!'

'Don't look, then. Keep your eyes on the road.'

Beyond the German positions, the first reserves of tanks waited, hidden among sand bunkers. Ahead of them was the confusion that Simon now knew and expected. The forward tanks had thrown up a screen of dust, blinding the drivers of vehicles in the rear. Lorries had bogged down in the soft sand and commanders were trying to guide their tanks round each obstruction as they came to it. They were lit by blazing vehicles that glowed through the dust like a stage effect. None of it was new to Simon. Seeing petrol leaking from a burning truck, he shouted to Crosbie: 'Make a dash for it before the whole show goes up and takes us with it.'

When they drove out of the dust belt, they found the moon had set and the overhanging face of the Fuka escarpment was just visible, darker than the prevailing darkness. Beneath it there was a gathering of torches where the tank commanders conferred. Simon, going forward on foot, reached the command tank as the sky grew pallid with first light.

The CO greeted him with little patience, saying as Simon handed him the map: 'What've you got there? Let's hope it makes sense because nothing else does. They call us a *corps de chasse* but how the hell can we chase anything with supply trucks littering the ground and now a ruddy mine field in the way.'

'It's a dummy, sir.'

'So they think, but I want to know more about it. We've lost seventeen tanks already, mostly on mines.'

'You can see it here, sir. Our chaps laid it in June when the retreat was on.'

'Damn fool thing to do.' The commander, in a fury, turned his back on Simon and Simon, in no better humour, went to the jeep, saying to himself, 'They might have let me sleep.'

He had only been gone ten minutes but Crosbie was unconscious over the wheel and Simon, with scarcely the heart to wake him, thought, 'Don't blame him, either,' then shouted, 'Come on, Crosbie, lazy bastard. For God's sake, let's get back to camp.'

9

Winter enlivened not only the human occupants of Garden City but the cockroaches that scuttled, as big as rats, round the skirting. A green praying mantis, four inches high, was found clinging to a curtain. Bats, delighting in their new vitality, began to visit the flat. One night three of them flew together through the open balcony door and out through the window at the other end of the room. Before anyone had recovered from his surprise, they were back through the window and out at the door, giving a playful skip in mid-flight as though they were playing a game.

Dobson thought they must be attracted by the light but Angela and Harriet said bats avoided light. No one expected to see them again but next evening, while the sky still held the glow of sunset, the bats returned. This time five came in a close line and at one point each did a little caracole that seemed a salute to the humans in the room.

For the next two nights there were no bats then three – perhaps the original three – darted in and out again. Bats came at intervals for nearly a fortnight. Harriet, who used to fear them, began to see them as guardian spirits and feel affection for them. Then, just when it seemed they had adopted the place, the visits ceased. Harriet could not believe they had gone for good and waited in to see them. When they did not come, she said to Angela, 'We are bereft.'

'We can go bat watching at the Union.'

That meant they would have to go in early evening when the

bats were most active and people could sit out for a little in the moist, mild air under the towering trees. In the officers' club opposite, the Egyptian officers also sat out at sunset, wearing their winter uniforms, but as soon as the evening star showed in the copper green after-glow, they gathered themselves together and went indoors. As the cold came down, Angela said, 'We should go in, too.'

Harriet, who had been watching the short, darting flight of the bats among the trees, sadly agreed: 'We might as well. They're not our bats. They don't know us.'

Angela laughed at her and stood up, eager to go in search of Castlebar.

Although the two women were not expected at that hour, Castlebar and Jackman reached the table almost as soon as the whisky bottle. Angela, laughing, pushed it towards them, pretending that that alone was the attraction.

Having set up his cigarette pack and lit a cigarette, Castlebar put his hand in his pocket and brought out the heart of rose-diamonds. He smiled at Angela, saying, 'Pin it on for me.'

Angela gave a little scream of shocked delight: 'You wouldn't dare!'

'Oh, wouldn't I?' Castlebar, his eye-tooth out to meet the challenge, glanced round to see who was watching him, and pinned the heart to his lapel then slid his hand under the table in search of Angela's hand, and so they sat with the heart between them.

Several people were watching them but Jackman looked the other way. Harriet thought he was showing disapproval but, following the direction of his gaze, she saw a short, heavy, square-built woman looking for someone among the tables. Her light clothing marked her as a newcomer whose blood had not been conditioned by the Egyptian summer. Jackman made no sign but his expression, a slightly malicious expression, suggested to Harriet that he knew who she was.

Catching sight of Castlebar, she came straight to him, watching him with a purposeful and sardonic smile. She called out, 'Hello, Wolfie!'

At the sound of her strong, carrying voice, Castlebar's eyes opened. Seeing who had spoken, his startled stare changed to alarm. He grew pale. Dropping Angela's hand as though he could not imagine what he was doing with it, he half lifted himself from the chair and tried to speak. His stammer increasing so he was barely intelligible, he began, 'M⁄m⁄m⁄Mona ... L⁄L⁄L⁄Lambkin!' then too shocked to support himself, he fell back and tried again: 'H⁄h⁄h⁄how ...'

'How did I get here?' Mona Castlebar's eyebrows rose in triumph. She placed a chair firmly at the table and sat upon it: 'By air, of course. Didn't you get my cable?'

'N⁄n⁄n⁄no.'

The company was silent, looking at this weighty woman who had once been Castlebar's Lambkin: then they saw the horror her arrival had roused in him. Of course there had been no cable. She had come without warning, intending to catch him in some misdeed, and she had caught him. With her sardonic smile fixed, she looked first at Harriet then at Angela, not sure which had been the lure. Returning to Castlebar, she said: 'What a splendid decoration! Is it meant for me?'

As she put out her hand to take the brooch, Angela, roused from her first dismay, spoke with spirit: 'No, it's not meant for you. It was a present for my friend Harriet here. Bill put it on for a joke.'

'Y⁄y⁄yes ... just a l⁄l⁄l⁄little joke.' Castlebar's fingers shook as he undid the brooch and handed it to Angela. Angela passed it to Harriet who put it into her handbag, then they all looked again at Mona Castlebar.

'Well, well!' she said and the rest were silent. She observed each in turn as though summing them up. She did not like them and she knew they did not like her. She met their antagonism with a bellicose smile.

Harriet wondered how any woman, newly arrived after a long journey, could seem so confidently in control of a situation. Did her appearance, perhaps, mask her diffidence? Harriet thought not. But, of course, she was not in a strange place. She had lived in Cairo before the war and had known exactly where to come to find her husband.

Her dress was cut to display her only attraction: fine shoulders and bosom. She was older than the others at the table, even older than Castlebar. Her square face with its short nose, small eyes and heavy chin, was already falling into lines. Newly arrived from a temperate climate, her pallor seemed ghastly to the others and it was accentuated by the unreal red of her hair.

Castlebar put out a hand for another cigarette and could scarcely lift it from the box. He poured himself the last of the whisky and his wife said, 'You've had about enough,' then added as one demanding her due: 'If anyone's buying another round, mine's a strong ale.'

'Now, Lambkin, you won't get strong ale here – you know that. Have this,' Castlebar pushed his glass across to her: 'Come on. Tell us how you got here.' His wheedling tone suggested a hope that somehow an explanation would send her back where she came from.

'You do want to know, don't you, Wolfie?'

He nodded and Harriet realised that 'Wolfie' was a reference to the tooth that overhung his lip when he was angry or when, as now, he was hopelessly at a loss.

Provokingly, she went, 'Hmmm,' as though about to tell but taking her time and then, apparently revealing something too precious to be lightly given away, she said: 'ENSA. They sent me out with a party.'

Neither Angela nor Castlebar had ever thought of ENSA. Angela glanced at him but he was careful not to glance at her.

Harriet asked, 'You sing, do you?'

'Of course. I'm a pro. Hasn't Bill told you about me?'

Evading the question, Harriet turned to Angela: 'Mrs Castlebar ought to meet Edwina as they're both singers. Perhaps we could arrange an evening?'

Angela did not reply. Castlebar nervously asked: 'Where are you staying, Lambkin?'

'With you, I hope.'

'Yes. Oh, yes. I just thought ENSA might be putting you up in style.'

'They probably would if I wanted it, but I don't intend having much truck with them.'

'Surely, if they brought you out . . .'

'Don't be soft, Wolfie. Now I'm here, they can't do anything. They can't send me back. I've got the laugh on them. Anyway, you know I've a sensitive larynx. Anything can upset it, so if I can't sing, I can't.' Mona emptied the glass as though to say, 'That's final,' then, fixing her yellow-brown eyes upon him, gave an order: 'Better get a move on, Wolfie. I left my bags at the ENSA office. We must pick them up, and I want to buy a few things. So come along.'

Castlebar rose, promptly but shakily, holding to the edge of the table. Instinctively, Angela rose with him and made to steady him, then drew her hand away, realising she had been displaced. Observing this movement, Mona stared at Angela with narrowed eyes. Angela had betrayed herself.

As the Castlebars went ahead, the others followed, having nothing else to do. Jackman, who had not spoken since Mona's appearance, stared at her back view and gave a snigger of contempt. Her short dress was made shorter by being stretched over her massive backside.

'Look at that woman's legs,' he said. 'They're solid wood. Not even a slit between them.'

Angela tried to smile but her misery was apparent. She walked with head hanging and Harriet took hold of her hand. They left the Union and went across the bridge to the taxi rank outside the Extase. Mona was already seated inside a taxi when they arrived and Castlebar, peremptory in his agitation and guilt, said to Angela, 'Got to call it a day. Have to collect the luggage . . . s-s-s-see her to the flat. She looks all in.'

'Does she?' Angela's tone was sullen but in spite of herself, she put a hand on Castlebar's arm and looked appealingly at him.

From inside the taxi came a warning call: 'Wolfie!'

'M-m-m-must go.' Castlebar sped from the company, fearing to be detained, and struggled into the taxi. Angela watched after it as it drove away.

Jackman, tittering, said to her: 'Think of it! There's only one bed at his place. He'll have to sleep with her.' When Angela did not reply, he asked: 'Where are we going now?'

She turned abruptly from him and put out her hand to Harriet: 'Nowhere. I'm tired. I want an early night.'

Abandoning Jackman, the two women walked slowly under the riverside trees towards Garden City.

'He won't stay with her long,' Harriet said.

'Perhaps not, but they've been married for twenty years. If he can't bear her (as he says) why didn't he leave her long ago?'

'He had no incentive. It's different now.' Harriet took the rose-diamond heart from her bag: 'Here's the brooch. At least, she didn't get that.'

'I gave it to you.'

'But you didn't mean me to keep it.'

'Yes. Why not? You like those stones. What good is it to me?'

'Thank you.' Harriet paused and holding the brooch cupped in her hand, looked at the diamonds catching the embankment lights: 'Thank you, Angela. I love it.'

A week passed without news of Castlebar. He may have gone to the Union but Angela would not go in search of him. She said to Harriet, 'He knows where I am. If he wants to see me, he can ring me,' but he did not ring.

Harriet, aware of Angela's disquiet, suggested they invite the Castlebars in: 'We said she should meet Edwina. So let's fix an evening!'

Angela, sprawled on the sofa, shrugged as though indifferent but, looking up, her expression brightened and she at once gave Harriet Castlebar's telephone number. 'If you want to ask them, it's all right with me.'

Harriet rang Castlebar's flat but there was no reply. She decided to settle the matter by going to the Union.

'Why not come with me? You've no reason to stay away.'

'No. I couldn't bear seeing him there with her.'

Harriet disliked appearing alone in public places but, feeling that any action was better than the dejection that kept Angela inactive, she sent Hassan out for a gharry. It was early in the evening and she expected to find Castlebar at the snooker table with Jackman, but there was no sign of Jackman. Castlebar was seated at a table with Mona beside him.

So there they were: Wolfie and Lambkin: the lamb and the wolf! Harriet went straight to them.

At the sight of her, Castlebar grinned and his grin was both feeble and defiant. He knew she condemned him for his neglect of Angela, but what could he do? His wife had whistled him back and now held him helpless in their old relationship. He looked trapped and ashamed of himself but prepared to bluster it out. Mona, in possession, was smugly conscious of the legality of her own position.

They seemed to expect Harriet to accuse them but Harriet was not there to make accusations. Uninvolved and apparently friendly, she offered them the invitation.

Mona, not expecting it, bridled slightly as though unsure how to deal with it, then answered in a lofty tone: 'I'm not sure. What are we doing that night, Wolfie? I think we're engaged.'

'Oh, Lambkin, of course we're not. Why shouldn't we go?'

'Very well, if you're so keen.'

Harriet said, 'Then you accept?'

Mona nodded a graceless, 'All right.'

Harriet, having come only for Angela's sake, refused the offer of a drink and left at once. Although she knew Angela would be on edge until she heard the result of her approach to the Castlebars, she walked back to Garden City. Having seen him in the grasp of his wife, she felt she had been unwise to foster Angela's infatuation with anyone so futile.

Angela was still lying on the sofa, her head buried in her arms. She jerked herself up as Harriet entered and demanded, 'Well?'

'It's all right. They've accepted.'

'So they were there? What were they doing?'

'Nothing much. Just sitting, drinking beer.'

'How did he look?'

'Not happy. I would say he was trapped.'

'Trapped? Ah!' Angela gave a long sigh of agonised relief then, throwing her arms into the air, she shrieked with a laughter that was very near hysteria.

Guy, when he heard that Mona Castlebar was a singer, became interested in the supper party and said, 'I'd like to ask Hertz and Allain.'

'Oh, darling, they wouldn't fit in.'

'Of course they'll fit in. They're well-mannered and agreeable and help out whenever needed. Everyone likes them. You couldn't find a nicer couple of guests.'

Dobson said, 'Wouldn't it be better to ask them on their own?'

'No, they'll get on with Castlebar. They'll have a lot in common.'

'Oh, well, if they're as charming as you say, I look forward to meeting them.'

Edwina agreed to be in to meet Mona but when the evening came, she said she was sorry, 'terribly, terribly sorry,' but Peter was taking her to supper at the Kit-Kat. As a result of this defection, Harriet felt more inclined to welcome Hertz and Allain.

They and Guy, having evening classes, were expected to arrive late. The Castlebars, with nothing to detain them, would probably be first. Angela, awaiting them, moved restlessly between the living-room and her bedroom, looking as though she might, at the sound of the doorbell, disappear altogether. Harriet said, 'Do sit down, Angela. Keep calm. When they come, don't let them see you're worried.'

Guy brought home the two men, both young and good-looking, with a muscular grace, like athletes in training, and Harriet hoped they would distract Angela, but Angela seemed scarcely aware of them. As time passed and no one else arrived, her vacant stare became more vacant. She had nothing to say.

The young men, refusing alcohol, drank iced lime-juice. Dobson, entertaining them with diplomatic ease, congratulated Guy on finding two such employees at such a time.

'You must be very fond of teaching,' he said to them.

Hertz and Allain appeared gratified by Dobson's attention. Carefully enunciating each word, Allain told him: 'Yes, we are very fond of teaching.'

'You see it as a vocation, no doubt?'

'A vocation, certainly. We see it as a vocation,' Allain looked to Hertz for confirmation and Hertz, as though eager to please, smiled and vigorously nodded his head.

Guy, delighted with both of them, would have been content to sit drinking and talking for the rest of the evening, but it was nearly nine o'clock. The food was ready and Hassan was lurking, aggrieved, in the doorway.

Harriet said, 'I think we'll have to eat.'

As they moved to the table, the front-door bell rang and Angela paused, paralysed by anticipation, Hassan, answering the door, came back with a telegram addressed to Harriet.

She read: 'Please excuse. Mona not too well, Bill.' and handed it to Angela who gave it a glance, dropped it on the floor and made for the baize door to the bedroom. Harriet called after her: 'Won't you have supper?'

'No, I'm not hungry.'

Guy, talking at the table, expressed his enthusiasm for a Jewish National Home in Palestine. He was particularly impressed by the idea of kibbutzim, based he believed on the Russian soviets, and the possibility of turning the Negev into arable land. The teachers, although Jews themselves, smiled politely but had, it seemed, no great interest in these ambitious schemes.

Dobson, who knew more that Guy did, discussed them from a practical viewpoint: 'It all sounds fine,' he said. 'But these things can't be carried out without money, a great deal of money. Well, the Jews have money – much of it comes from the States – and they can buy tractors and fertilisers and combined harvesters, while the wretched Arabs are still scraping the ground with the same ploughs they used in biblical times. They'd go on doing this, quite happily, if they weren't made envious by the equipment the Jews have got. As it is, they are resentful and likely to make trouble, so, to keep them sweet, HMG has to fork out to give them tractors and pedigree bulls and other rich gifts . . .'

'But this is magnificent,' Guy broke in. 'Thanks to the Jews, the Arabs are being provided for.'

'My dear fellow, it has to be paid for. And who pays? The poor, old British tax-payer. As per usual.'

'Oh, come, Dobbie! You surely don't object to a rich country like Britain helping the poor Palestinians?'

Dobson laughed: 'I don't object, but your Jewish friends do.'

Reminded of his guests, Guy was quick to defend the Jews: 'I don't believe it. I'm sure they don't object. It's up to all of us to share the sum of human knowledge and advance the under-developed peoples of the world.' His eyes glowing with faith in all-pervading human goodness, he looked to Hertz and Allain for support, and they both solemnly nodded their agreement with his sentiments. It looked like dispassionate agreement but Harriet, who had watched them while they were listening to Guy, had seen on their faces an intent expression that did not accord with their apparent detachment from the subject in hand.

Guy pursued it, fervently postulating ethics that Dobson good-humouredly amended, while Harriet, not much interested in polemics, waited for a chance to go to Angela. When she went to the room, she found her lying in darkness, made more dark by a large mango tree that blotted out most of the sky.

Harriet said, 'Shall I put on the light?'

'No.'

Harriet sat on the edge of the bed: 'This is Mona's doing, of course.'

'Yes, but he let her do it,' Angela raised herself on her elbow. 'He's frightened of her and she despises him. She despises him, yet she'll keep her hold on him simply to prevent anyone else getting him. Her "Wolfie"! – God help us! Harriet, what's the cure for love?'

'Another love.'

'Not so easy. You want one person, not another. I must get away for a while. I don't want to go to the Union – which I will, sooner or later, if I stay here. So I must go where he isn't. I want to be out of sight. I want to get away from him. The truth is: he's a dead loss.'

'Where can you go?'

'I've been thinking. When I was with Desmond, we used to spend every winter in Luxor. I could go back there. Would you come with me?'

'I don't know, I'll have to see what we have in the bank.'

'Don't be silly, it's my treat.'

'No. It can't always be your treat.'

'Well, it is this time, And what the hell does it matter? I can afford it. If you come to please me, why shouldn't it be my treat?'

They argued it out and agreed that Angela should pay for the train journey but Harriet would settle her own hotel bill. By now it was taken for granted that they would go to Luxor and Angela, seeing herself escaping from an obsession, became excited and putting her arms about Harriet, she promised her, 'We'll have a riotous time. We'll see everything there is to see down there. We'll go to a hotel with the best food in Egypt. We'll live it up, and to hell with bloody Bill Castlebar and his even bloodier wife.'

Angela's euphoria remained with her on the train to Luxor. When they were in the dining-car, she ordered a bottle of whisky although she would be the only one to drink it. In flight from Castlebar, she could talk of nothing but Castlebar – and Castlebar's wife. She had heard at Groppi's, where she sometimes took tea with friends from her married days, that Mona Castlebar was already a subject for gossip. She had been invited to a musical evening arranged by the American University in aid of the Red Cross. Edwina was also invited and both women were expected to sing for the cause. Edwina complied willingly, sing-ing song after song, until she became aware of Mona's critical stare, at which she broke off and turning to Mona, said, 'But I'm being selfish. I must stop. It's your turn now.'

'And what do you think?' Angela squealed with delight: 'Mona refused to sing. She seemed to think she was being tricked into performing and she said "I only do it for money".'

'Did she really say that?'

'Well, no.' In the face of Harriet's disbelief, Angela moderated her story: 'What she actually said was "I don't give my services free". *Her services*! Heaven help us!'

As Angela paused in her laughter to wipe her eyes, Harriet asked: 'Was Bill there?'

'Yes. And they say he was horribly embarrassed and begged her to sing "just one little *Lieder*" – *Lieder*'s her thing – but she wouldn't, and there she sat on her big bottom, in a long green dress, with that mantelpiece of a bosom sticking out of it, her face grim, as obstinate as a pig. No one could get a squeak out of her.'

'How did Bill come to marry such a woman in the first place?'

'Oh, he's a simple soul. She paraded the bosom and kept the legs out of sight. He told me he thought she was "the Great Earth Mother", now he says she's a lout. Yet she's only got to turn up and he's at her heels. It makes me sick.'

'He'll rebel sooner or later.'

'Too late for me. I've finished with him.' Angela emptied her glass and put the cap back on the bottle. 'This'll do for tomorrow.' Her merriment had started to flag – and a desperate merriment it was, Harriet thought. She looked haggard and weary and said, 'Let's go to bed.'

They had first-class sleepers and slept well, but next morning the excursion took on a different aspect. At breakfast in the dining-car, Angela would take nothing but coffee and had little to say. They looked out of the window at the disturbing sight of graves beside the track, dozens of them, each one a mound of sand with a palm leaf stuck at the head. The train was running through a cemetery and at stations, where a lively crowd usually gathered to gape at the tourists, the platforms were deserted except for a few forlorn villagers who stood about listlessly with dejected eyes.

Angela, to whom Upper Egypt was well known, could make nothing of this desolation. And the graves continued: new graves, not simply dozens of them but hundreds. She called a waiter and spoke to him in Arabic then translated his reply: 'He says there's been an epidemic and many people have died.'

'But of what?'

'He doesn't know. He just says "a bad sickness".'

'Why weren't we told about this? There was nothing in the papers. Ask him why it was kept secret.'

The waiter, a small, light-coloured man with a gentle face,

was unable to answer this question. He knew nothing of news-
papers and the deceits of governments, but his expression as he
looked from the window was uneasy and Harriet, seeing the other
waiters gathered at the end of the car, said, 'They're all frightened.'
The visitors came here in ignorance but the waiters came because
they could not afford to refuse.

The few officers and nurses at the other tables seemed un-
affected by the conditions outside the train. Seeing that one of the
men wore the insignia of a medical officer, Angela called to him,
'Doctor, what's the matter here? The whole place is a graveyard.'

The doctor, looking out, appeared to see the graves for the first
time. 'Rum go,' he said and shouted for the head waiter. Why, he
wanted to know, had the epidemic not been reported to the army?

'Hotels want people to come,' the head waiter earnestly
explained.

'They do, do they? And what have they got here? Plague,
smallpox, spotted fever? – some little thing like that?'

The head waiter grinned. Taking the doctor's angry humour
for facetiousness, he tried to make light of the trouble: 'It is nothing.
It is a thing they have here.'

The doctor's tone changed: 'Come on, what is it?'

Challenged by this important-sounding officer, the head waiter
went back to his subordinates and they conferred together. He
returned to say: 'Malaria, effendi. Not too bad. You take quinine,
you all very well.'

The doctor rejected malaria and made his own decision. He
told his fellow diners: 'It's probably cholera. Nothing to worry
about if you're careful. Eat only cooked food, and eat it hot.
Avoid tap water, salads, fresh fruit. Drink bottled spring water.
French, if you can get it.'

Reassured, Harriet and Angela began to discuss the dangers of
life in the Middle East. Harriet told how she had danced at the
Turf Club with an officer who was sickening for smallpox.
Angela, becoming more animated, said she had been to a dinner-
party where a certain Major Beamish was expected but did not
arrive: 'Then another guest, an MO, said, "I did a PM on a chap
called Beamish this morning" and the host said "It couldn't be

our Beamish. He was alive and well when we saw him last night." But it was their Beamish. While we waited for him, he was in his grave, dead in the night of poliomyelitis.'

Harriet had never heard of poliomyelitis. Angela said, 'If you get it here, it hits you hard. You're gone in no time.' Though she essayed this information herself, it had a dire effect upon her. She sat silent, staring out at the graves and the palm fronds that were drying and turning yellow. Soon they would be blown away and the graves with them. They would be sifted by the wind, one into the other, until the ground was flat again and the dead forgotten. She whispered, 'People can die so suddenly,' and she was distraught by her own fancies.

They drew into Luxor. Outside the station, a funeral was passing: a flimsy, open coffin held aloft by four men, was followed by the family and professional mourners who enacted grief by howling and throwing dust over their heads.

Angela, about to call a gharry, stopped and said, 'Harriet, I can't stay. I must go back.'

'Oh, Angela, surely you're not afraid?'

'Not for myself – of course not. I just can't bear being so far from Bill. Anything might happen to him. Suppose he died in the night as Beamish did?'

'It's not very likely. And even if you went back: what could you do? What difference would it make?'

'Only that I was there. I would be near him, not four hundred miles away.'

Harriet tried to reason with her: 'Be sensible, Angela. Beamish was only one person. Think of all the English people who haven't died here, so why should Bill be in peculiar danger?'

'In this place, we're all in peculiar danger. Any one of us might die any minute.' Angela's face, with its delicate, dry skin, was taut with fear, and Harriet saw that reasoning was useless. Even if she could be persuaded to stay, she would be miserable. Persuading her against her will would be a cruelty.

Harriet, reconciling herself to their return, said, 'Very well. If we must go back, we must. Let's find when the train goes.'

'No, not you. You must stay. I'll go alone. It doesn't matter about me, I've seen all the sights, I know the place inside and out. But it's all new to you. You must stay and enjoy it.'

Harriet, who had no wish to enjoy it alone, tried to argue but Angela insisted that Harriet remain in Luxor while she went back to Cairo. Finding that the train would not return until late in the evening, she decided to go to the hotel with Harriet. She must wait for time to pass.

Angela had booked them into the old Winter Palace, a pleasant building beside the Nile, its portico heavily embowered with verdure, its terrace overhung by palms.

The day was still early, the light pale and the soft, cool air scented by some flowering tree. Harriet said, 'What a delightful place,' and driving in the gharry, silent on the sandy roads, she longed for Angela to remain with her. But the funerals, passing one after the other, aggravated Angela's nervous condition. She explained to Harriet that only the bodies were buried, the coffins were kept to be used again. Some of them, padded, draped and fringed, denoted victims from affluent families but others had been too poor even to hire a coffin. The bodies, closely wrapped in cloth, were carried on a board with a symbol to denote the sex: a fez for the male and a flow of hair for the female. But each, whether rich or poor, male or female, had its dusty crew of women mourners, the wails of one procession scarcely fading before those of another could be heard.

The piercing ululations followed Harriet and Angela even into the haven of the hotel. As they sat under the palms, watching the traffic on the narrow waterway between the quay and the island opposite, Angela was too distracted even to order a drink. Seeing her with her face set in a mask of suffering, Harriet knew she was thinking of her son, a beautiful boy for whose death she had, in a way, been responsible. In those days she had painted pictures and while she was too intent on her work to notice, he had picked up a live grenade which had exploded in his hand.

As she remembered this, Harriet could understand Angela's state of mind. After such a tragedy, how could she trust anyone to remain alive? – least of all Castlebar whom she loved and longed for.

They went in to luncheon where, for a while, she discussed the question of what they should or should not eat, but this did not last long. Throwing the menu aside, she said, 'What does it matter? If I could die, it would be the easiest way out.'

Somehow they got through the day. After supper, the gharry called as arranged and Harriet, glad of something to do, went with Angela to the station. At the station, she made a last appeal: 'Don't you think you could stay for a couple of days?'

'No. I'm sorry, Harriet. I know it's mean to leave you alone here. But I must go back.'

There was no one else in the first-class compartment. Angela was given a berth in a long row of empty berths and, standing in the doorway, she said, 'Don't wait, Harriet. Goodbye,' then shut herself in to suffer through the night.

As she returned in the gharry to the hotel, an intense loneliness came down on Harriet. At that time of night, the streets were empty, the river empty of shipping. The gharry driver, and the horse plodding silently through silence, seemed to be the only other creatures in a deserted world.

Above the low houses the sky appeared vast and its great staring but indifferent expanse enhanced the solitude. Her bed-room, when she reached it, looked as void as the town. It was very large and her bed, shrouded in a sand-fly net, was islanded in the middle of the floor. Getting into it and covering herself with a sheet and a single blanket, she closed the net against the dangers of the night. Angela's flight had reduced her to a sense of friendlessness but as she lay down to sleep, she, too, said, 'What does it matter?' though she did not intend to die. Instead, she said, 'I've survived other things. I'll survive this,' and so went to sleep.

The desk clerk offered her a number of sight-seeing trips and she accepted them all. The first started immediately after breakfast. The tourists gathered beneath the riverside palms in air so cool, it seemed to blow off the sea. Harriet thought, 'Paradise must be like this,' then the funerals started again. Those who had died during the night must be buried before the heat of mid-day.

A string of gharries stood outside the hotel. Harriet, seated alone in the first of them, found funerals passing beside her. She could look into the open coffins and see the dark, peaked faces of people who appeared to have died of starvation. This went on until the dragoman, appearing to take charge of the tourists, ordered the mourners to the other side of the road. They shifted ground without protest and without a pause in their lamentations.

The dragoman, complacent in his authority, was a large Nubian, his size enhanced by a full, dark blue kaftan, lavishly trimmed with gold. His stick was taller and heavier than those usually carried and it was topped by an ivory head as big as a skull. He chose to ride in Harriet's gharry and though he sat beside the driver, it was evident he saw himself as superior to the members of the party.

The gharries went from hotel to hotel, picking up nurses and army officers. At the last hotel there was only one person waiting, an officer, and as he, too, was alone, he was directed by the dragoman to the leading gharry. He paused, his foot on the step, and staring at Harriet, asked, 'Are you real? – or have I conjured you out of a dream?'

It was a rhetorical question, expressively spoken, and Harriet laughed at it: 'Get in, Aidan. If I'd never seen you before, I would have known you were an actor.'

'*Was* an actor,' the officer corrected her as he sat down beside her. On the London stage he had taken the name of Aidan Sheridan but in the army had reverted to his real name which was Pratt. He was a captain in the Pay Corps, based in Syria but as often as he could, came to Egypt on duty or pleasure. In the past, Harriet had heard him speak bitterly of his broken career but that morning his tone was one of humorous resignation to his present position.

As soon as he could without appearing precipitant, he asked, 'I suppose Guy isn't with you?'

It was the question Harriet expected. When he came to Cairo, it was in hope of seeing Guy, and though she pitied him, she could only say, 'I'm afraid not.'

'So you're here alone?'

'I didn't come alone, but I'm alone now. I was abandoned.'

He gave her a startled glance, suspecting some interrupted liaison, and she laughed again: 'A woman friend came with me, but at the sight of the funerals, she went straight back to Cairo.'

'I can't say I blame her. I, too, felt scared when I realised what was going on here.'

'Oh, Angela wasn't scared, at least not for herself. She began thinking of death – someone else's death – and she couldn't bear to stay.'

Aidan, aware that the only death he had thought of was his own, grew red and, taking her words for a reprimand, turned away. She had forgotten how easy it was to upset him and regretted what she had said. He was morbidly sensitive but, more than that, he had been marked by some experience that he promised one day to reveal to her. He was a young man, still in his mid-twenties, but his large, dark eyes were set in hollows of dark skin and their expression suggested a rooted unhappiness. They had seldom met yet they had become friends. She had taken him to the Muski where he had bought a small votive cat made of iron and mounted on a block of cornelian. It was a gift for his mother but he had asked Harriet to keep it for him, saying he lost things because he no longer had the sense that anything was worth keeping. Speaking of the experience that had so terribly impaired him, he had said, 'There are some memories that are beyond bearing, except that we have to bear them.'

Now, meeting him again in this delectable place, she saw he was still burdened by a memory beyond bearing.

A long, riverside road was leading them to the site of Karnac. The gharries stopped outside the walls and the dragoman, walking impressively, led his party into a compound and, making a circular movement with his stick, required its members to stand about him at a respectful distance. He pointed to the temple of Ammon.

'This am very great place. Biggest building in the world. This avenue is sphinxes, only not sphinxes. They is sheep.'

'Rams, surely?' Aidan murmured.

Ignoring him, the dragoman swept round like a whirling

dervish and strode towards the main complex of buildings: 'You alls follow me.'

In the Hypostyle Hall, while the others were held by a rig-marole about Ramses XII, Harriet slid behind the group and made her way among the crowded pillars that stood, calm but watchful, like trees in a forest. She felt that their number and closeness were designed to puzzle, for apart from puzzlement she could see little point in congestion simply for congestion's sake. As for the puzzle: she had the curious illusion that she had, at one time, solved it but had forgotten the solution. Gazing up at the capitals, she saw that only some of them were bud capitals, the others were decorated with the papyrus calyx, and she imagined that in the irregular placing of these two designs there was a clue to the mystery. But the heat was growing and as she wandered about, all she could feel was wonderment without hope of understanding.

Aidan, coming to look for her, said, 'Our dragoman's a mine of misinformation. I'm not surprised you made off. Come with me. The sun's almost overhead – there's something I want to show you.'

She followed him out to the courtyard and across to a small building that was lit by a hagioscope in the front wall. Putting his eye to the hole, Aidan smiled his satisfaction then gestured to her to come and look for herself. She, too, put her eye to the hole and saw inside, lit by a shaft of sunlight from the roof, the head of a cat. It was the same cat whose image Aidan had bought in the Muski but this was more than life-size, a black basalt head on top of a column, gazing with remote, mild gaze into its own eternal seclusion.

'The god in the sanctuary.'

'Yes,' Aidan looked pleased: 'I thought you would recognise it.'

The afternoon excursion was to the tombs on the other side of the river. Crossing in a boat, Harriet felt on her bare head, a pressure that was almost painful, and she realised how soon the respite of winter would be over and this paradisal little town would become an inferno for those not born to it.

On the opposite bank, in a field that had once been inundated by the Nile, two ruined figures sat enthroned among the sugar beet. Their dark colour, their immense height, their worn and featureless faces looking towards Karnac, imparted such an impression of regal dignity, Harriet would have chosen to contemplate them in silence. The dragoman was not permitting that.

'Them, all two, is Memnon, not singing any more. Memnon very brave Greek man killed in battle. Him buried here.'

Aidan said, 'Nonsense.'

A nurse with a guide book agreed. 'It says here they're statues of Amenophis III.'

The dragoman stood in front of nurse and book as though to obliterate them and pushed his face towards Aidan. His eyes, brown, in balls of glossy white, started in anger from their sockets. He shouted, 'You is guide, then, Mister Officer? OK. You go guide your own self. I finish. I go.'

He swept off and went at a furious pace back to the river's edge but there had to stop. The ferry had returned to Luxor.

The nurse, dismayed by his departure, said to the others, 'Oh dear! I didn't mean to hurt his feelings. Should I go and tell him I'm sorry? I might persuade him to come back.'

Before anyone else could speak, Aidan, assuming an ironical air of authority, said, 'Certainly not. He doesn't know his arse from his elbow. We're better off without him,' and the others, impressed by the act, let themselves be conducted to where some donkeys and old taxis stood ready to take them into the Valley of the Kings. The drivers, seeing the dragoman dismissed, were jubilant while the dragoman himself, realising what was happening, came running back, bawling at the top of his voice, 'You no go without guide. Law say no one go without guide,' but the tourists were already in the taxis and the drivers, gleefully starting up, were away before he reached them. While he raged behind them, they went bumping and swaying up the rocky track to the valley where the kings and queens of Upper and Lower Egypt had left their earthly remains.

On the quay, when they returned there, Aidan asked Harriet if she would have dinner with him that evening. It was arranged that she should go to his hotel by gharry but the evening was so pleasant, she decided to walk. The sun was setting in a lustre of crimson and gold and the Nile, small compared with the great river of Cairo, ran in loops of coloured light under the brilliant sky. She paused to look down into the walled hollow that held the Temple of Luxor. There was a mosque among the jumble of remains and a man, probably the attendant, looked up, grinning, and said, 'Ghost, ghost.' He seemed to expect her to run and was disconcerted when she leant over the wall and asked, 'Is there *really* a ghost?' but he could only repeat, 'Ghost, ghost,' and she laughed and went down to the quayside to walk under the palms.

The terrace of Aidan's hotel was built out over the water and served as a dining-room. It was roofed with greenery but closely netted against flying creatures and insects. One end was open to reveal the evening colours of the river but the inner area was shadowed and candles, their flames motionless inside tulip shades of engraved glass, were on the tables. There were less than a dozen diners, senior officers and their women, but the menu that Aidan held in front of his face was of a size that might have catered for a hundred. Hearing Harriet arrive beside him, he looked suspiciously round it, then, reassured by the sight of her, he put it down. He had placed a lily beside her plate, a white blaze bigger than the evening star, its central petals tied into a cone with thread. She knew he was trying to be gallant, but it was not easy for him. Yet they were oddly in sympathy, both wanting the same person and wishing he were here.

Aidan said, 'How about lobster? The waiter tells me it was flown in this morning from Aqaba.'

The lobster, when it came, was cold under a mayonnaise sauce and Harriet thought it delicious until she realised the danger of eating it. She put her fork down, her appetite gone, and Aidan asked with concern, 'Are you all right? I thought you looked strained, and you've lost weight, haven't you? How do you feel?'

'Not well. In fact, I gave up feeling well when I came to this country. Guy eats anything and everything, and he's never ill. I am careful with food and yet my inside's always upset.'

'Egypt is unpredictable. You never know what it will do to you. I hated it at first, then it grew on me. It's like a mother you detest, yet are tied to in spite of yourself. I think it's the place where we all began. It's here where we were born first and lived out the infancy of the soul.'

Harriet was surprised, not by what he had said but the fact he had said it, then she laughed: 'So you believe in reincarnation? Which pharaoh were you?'

Aidan did not laugh. He seemed affronted for a moment, then, remembering she was Guy's wife, he did his best to smile. Because she was Guy's wife, he had been happy to find her in Luxor, he had invited her to dinner and now he permitted her to laugh at him.

She responded by asking seriously: 'Is that why you are drawn to Egypt? Would you stay on here after the war?'

'Oh, no, it's too far from the centre of things. If you're an actor, you have to live in the world.'

'And this isn't the world?'

'Not my world, though I am, as you say, drawn to it. I intend to see what I can of it while I'm out here. Tomorrow I'm going to Assuan to visit the gardens of Elephantine. They're so ancient, they were there when Alexander came to Egypt three hundred years before Christ.'

'What is Elephantine? An oasis?'

'No, an island in the river. It's called Elephantine because some king or other sacrificed an elephant there.'

'Sacrificed an elephant? How abominable!'

'It would be dead by now, anyway. It was a long time ago.' He laughed to show her he was being humorous and when she smiled, he said, 'Why don't you come to Assuan tomorrow?'

'I can't,' Harriet's money did not allow for a visit to Assuan. Angela, with her usual belief that the dearest thing was the cheapest in the end, had chosen one of the most expensive hotels in Luxor. Harriet said, 'I can't stay long.'

Aidan sighed enviously: 'I suppose Guy wants you back.'

Not sure what to say to that, Harriet smiled and Aidan, sympathising with her uncertainty, said he would walk with her to her hotel. They stopped by a row of small riverside shops that sold Egyptian antiquities and African curios. Although it was nearly midnight and there were few customers these days, the windows were lit and the owners still inside. Aidan bent down, intently examining objects made of ebony or of ivory trimmed with gold. Harriet wondered if he were thinking of a gift for his mother and reminded him: 'You know, I still have that little cat you bought in the Muski!'

'A cat? Yes, I did buy a cat, but what did I do with it?'

'You gave it to me to keep till you asked for it.'

'So I did. Yes, so I did.'

They left the shops and came to the Temple of Luxor. Harriet said, 'A man told me there is a ghost here'. They leant against the wall and peered down into darkness but no ghost moved through it. She said, 'You said you had lost the sense that anything was worth keeping. You said that one day you would tell me what caused it. Suppose you tell me here and now, while it's dark and I can't see your face!'

'I don't know . . . I don't think I can tell you.' He hung his head over the temple site that was like a pit of darkness where nothing could be discerned except a faint star-glimmer on one of the colossi of Ramses ii. When it seemed he had nothing more to say, she urged him:

'Whatever it was: if you keep it to yourself, you'll never get over it.'

'I don't expect to get over it. But what happened has no bearing on life as we know it. The dead are dead. There's nothing to be done about it now.'

'You mean, you don't want to tell me?'

'There's no reason why I shouldn't tell you. It's not a secret. It's only that I feel . . . I feel it's unjust to burden another person with the story.'

'Enough has happened to me. I don't need to be protected. And you promised.'

'Yes, that's true. I did promise,' he considered this fact for some minutes before saying, 'It's not what happened to me: that wasn't important. It's what happened to other people, most of them children.'

'That made it more terrible, of course.'

'More terrible, yes. And yet I don't know. As we have to die sooner or later, does it matter when we die?'

Leaving that question to answer itself, Harriet waited and eventually he went on: 'It was early in the war and I had declared myself a conscientious objector. I thought, being an actor, they might let me go on with my own work but, instead, I was directed on to a ship going to Canada. I had to act as a steward and waiter. I suppose the idea was to humiliate me. The other stewards were lascars, but we got on all right. In fact, I was rather enjoying the trip. There was a crowd of kids on board, being evacuated to Canada . . .'

'I think I can guess which ship that was. You were torpedoed?'

'Yes, just when we thought we were out of range of the U-boats. Our escorts had turned back. We took that to mean we were safe but the truth was, they turned back because they had used their quota of fuel. As soon as we were hit, the convoy scattered. That was according to orders. Whatever happened, the other ships had to save themselves and we were left to sink or swim. We were holed in the side and there was no hope for the ship itself. We had to get the kids into the boats and quick about it. We were going down fast. We tried to be cheerful – told the kids it was an adventure and we'd be picked up in no time. But there was no one to pick us up. It was a miserable night, cold, blowing a gale, pouring with rain. When daylight came, the convoy had vanished and there was no sign of the other boats. We were alone on the Atlantic. Nothing to be seen but the grey, empty sea. Absolutely alone.' Aidan paused to swallow in his throat, then he asked, 'Do you want to hear any more?'

'Of course.'

'The children were in their night clothes. We'd got them into life-jackets but when we realised how bad things were, there was no time to go down for blankets. The storm went on, the sea slapping up on us so there was a foot of bilge water in the boat. The kids were seasick but everyone was packed together so they couldn't get to the side. No one could move. There were nineteen children in our boat and two women helpers, volunteers. Then there were the lascars, fourteen of them. . . . And there was an elderly man who was joining his wife in Canada. We had one of the officers with us, a retired navy man who'd been recalled to active service. Kirkbride. He was splendid. Without him, we'd all have died. He knew how to propel the boat, which no one else did. There were no oars. Instead, there were handles like beer-pulls that had to be worked backwards and forwards. We tried to put the lascars on to that job but all they would do was pray and beseech Allah to rescue them. Not that it mattered. There was nowhere to go. We had no idea where we were. Kirkbride said he could navigate by the stars, but there were no stars. Only the black sky and the sea and the wind howling round us. God, the cold! It was bitterly cold. I'll never forget it.'

'Did you have any special job?'

'I doled out the food, what there was of it. There were iron rations in the boat: some tinned stuff and water. Not enough water. By the fourth day the ration was one mouthful of water and a sardine or a bit of bully on a ship's biscuit. The women did what they could to keep the kids amused – played games: "Animal, vegetable and mineral", that sort of thing, and got them to sing "Run rabbit" and "Roll out the barrel". The old man told them stories. Then one night one of the women dis-appeared; no one knew what happened to her. The water ran out and the kids couldn't swallow the biscuits because their throats were dry. I'd saved some condensed milk to the last but that wouldn't go down, either: it was too thick. After we'd been in the boat a week, the lascars gave up and began to die . . .'

Aidan stopped again and startled Harriet by laughing. She said 'Yes?'

'The storm got worse. We threw the dead lascars overboard and the waves threw them back again. We pretended this was funny but the kids had lost interest. They were dying, too. We always knew when a boy or girl was about to die, the kid would start having visions. One of them described an island covered with trees and kept pointing and saying, "Look, it's just over there. Why don't we go there?" Several times one of them would think he saw a ship coming to rescue us and the others would say they saw it, too.'

'I suppose they died of thirst?'

'Thirst and exposure. Their feet would go numb, then they'd sink into a coma and that was the end. Each morning, we'd find two or three of them dead. We used the tins to collect rainwater but it wasn't enough. After about ten days – I'd lost count by then – the second woman died. She'd wrapped her coat round one of the dying girls and she died herself. Hypothermia. Next day the last two children died. There was no one left but Kirk-bride, the old man, three of the lascars and me. We'd had nothing to eat for a week. The rain stopped so we hadn't even rainwater. We decided we'd had it and Kirkbride began to wonder where the boat would be cast up. He thought Iceland or the Faroes, but we knew it would probably just break up and no one would know what had happened to any of us. We'd rigged up a shelter for the smallest children and when there were no children left, we took it in turns to sleep there. The last time I crawled in, I said to myself "Thank God, I needn't wake up again!"'

Aidan's voice broke and Harriet, seeing the outline of the Ramses statue, wondered what it was doing there out in the dark Atlantic. After a long pause, she said, 'But that wasn't the end of the story?'

'Not quite, no. Kirkbride didn't go to sleep. He stayed on watch and he was awake when a Sunderland flew over us and dived to see what we were. He stood up and waved his shirt and they dropped us a tin of peaches. He woke me up . . . forced me back from another world by pouring peach juice down my throat. The Sunderland radioed all the ships anywhere near – I think the nearest was two hundred miles away – and the first one that reached us, picked us up.'

'And they were all alive: Kirkbride, the old man and the lascars?'

'Yes, I was the only one who died. And I should have stayed dead like the poor little brats we threw overboard. Some of them too light to sink. It was ghastly, seeing them floating after us. I should have died. Instead I woke up, safe and warm, in a bunk on board an American destroyer. The very smell of peach juice makes me sick . . .' Aidan pushed himself away from the wall and said in disgust: 'Now, you've heard it. That's the whole story.' He had told it in a flat voice with none of the dramatic force of his profession. The story itself was enough.

Harriet said, 'And you ceased to be a conscientious objector?'

'God, yes. One experience of that sort and I realised I'd be safer in the Pay Corps.'

His bitterness kept her silent and she told herself she would never laugh at him again.

As they walked on to Harriet's hotel, he regained his composure and saying 'goodnight', he took her hand and persuasively asked, 'Why not come to Assuan tomorrow?'

'I'm afraid it's impossible.'

'Then what about Damascus? You thought you might visit me there.'

'I would if I could persuade Guy to come with me.'

'Yes, *do* persuade him!' In his eagerness for Guy's company, he took a step towards her: 'And don't forget to remember me to him.'

'I'll give him your love,' Harriet said as she went into the hotel, and she realised she was laughing at him again.

Harriet's money ran out. There was nothing left for her to see in Luxor so she returned to Cairo a day earlier than expected. When she reached the flat, it was pervaded by an empty silence and she went to Angela's room in the hope of finding her there. Angela, too, was out but her suitcases were there, piled so high under the window they partly hid the mango tree that stared into the room.

Harriet went to her room and, lying on her bed, listened for someone to come in. She did not expect Guy, who seldom ate luncheon, but Angela, Edwina and Dobson were likely to arrive. She could imagine Angela laughing at the folly of her flight back to Cairo, or perhaps rejoicing because Castlebar had discovered he needed her. As for Harriet: all she wanted was a sense of welcome and an assurance that she was not as ill as she felt.

The bedrooms, barely tolerable in summer, were now cool but

the wood that had been baked and rebaked during the hot weather, still gave out a smell like ancient bone. From the garden outside the window came the herbal smell of dried foliage and the hiss of the hoses. She had been repeatedly wakened during the night by the railway servants who were under orders to spray the berths with disinfectant. She had argued that this was no way to prevent the spread of cholera but that did not stop them rapping on her door until she opened it. Half asleep on her bed, she heard a sound of sobbing and knew it came from the room of that other suffering lover: Edwina. She sat up with the intention of going to her, then realised she was not alone. Peter Lisdoonvarna, with joking gruffness, was telling her to 'shut up'. The sobbing grew louder and gave rise to a slap and scuffle and Peter's voice, contused with sexual intent, spoke hoarsely: 'Come on, you little bitch. Turn over.'

Harriet pushed her bedside chair so it crashed against the door, but the noise did not interrupt the lovers who, with squeaks, grunts and a rhythmic clicking of the bed, were locked together until Peter gave out a final groan and there was an interval of quiet before Edwina, in honeyed appeal, said, 'Teddy-bear, *darling*, you don't really mean to go back to the desert?'

'Fear so, old girl. Damned lucky to get back. Thought I was stuck in that God-damn office for the rest of the war.'

'Oh, Peter!' Edwina's wail was anguished but it was also resigned. She knew she could not prevent Peter going back to the desert but behind her appeals there was covert intention. She changed her tone as she said: 'When I passed the Cathedral yesterday, there was a military wedding and I waited to see them come out. The bridegroom was a major and the bride looked gorgeous. Her dress must have come from Cicurel's. I *did* envy her. I'd love to be married in the Cathedral.'

'In that yellow edifice beside Bulacq Bridge? You must be right off your rocker.'

'Well, where else is there?'

'I don't know. I've never thought about it.'

Peter's indifference to the subject was evident and Harriet wished she, too, could tell Edwina to 'shut up'. But time was short and Edwina was desperate. However unwise it was, she had to force the pace: 'Teddy-bear, darling, before you go . . .' she paused then rushed her proposal: '*Do* let's get married!'

There was a creaking noise as Peter got off the bed. Abrupt with embarrassment, he said, "Fraid I can't do that. Sorry. Blame m'self. Know I should have told you sooner, but didn't want to spoil things. Been a brute. Not fair to you. Didn't realise you cared in that way.'

'*Peter*! You're not married already?'

"Fraid so, old girl. Married m'cousin, Pamela. Great girl. Childhood sweethearts.'

'But how could you be married? People would know. Dobson would have told me.'

'Oh, I see. You think it was a big affair: St Margaret's, fully choral, dozen bridesmaids and pictures in the *Tatler*? Well, it was nothing like that. Didn't tell a soul. Just slipped into the Bloomsbury Registry Office and then had a week-end at Brown's. Only the family knew. With a war on, who cared, anyway?'

'But, Peter, there were dozens of marriages like that and they're breaking up all the time.'

'Perhaps, but I'm not breaking up this one. Pamela and I always knew we would marry. It's the real thing. So, be sensible. No reason why we shouldn't go on being friends.'

Edwina began to sob again, no doubt thinking that with Peter at the front and the British advancing towards Libya, there would not be much scope for friendship. Touched by her tears, Peter became impatient.

'Oh, come on, old girl! We've had a lot of fun, haven't we? Don't make a fuss now it's over.'

At the words 'it's over', Edwina broke down completely. Peter, unable to bear her violent weeping, opened the bedroom door and Harriet heard him mumbling as he went: 'Got to go, old girl. Sorry and all that. See you some time. 'Bye, 'bye.' He made off, his steps heavy in the corridor, then was gone, banging the front door after him. The departure was conclusive and Edwina was left to cry herself sick.

Knowing no way to comfort her, Harriet took herself out of

hearing. When Dobson came in, he found her lying on the sofa in the living-room and said, 'Hello, you safely back?'

'Not really. I feel worse than usual. Dobbie, it couldn't be cholera, could it?'

He had, of course, heard about the cholera from Angela. Harriet felt, rather than saw, his movement away from her and felt his fear that she had brought the disease into the flat. Still, he did his best to reassure her.

'When I heard there was an epidemic down there, I made enquiries and was told there was no cholera anywhere in Egypt. The minister said there had been an outbreak of food poisoning in the south.'

'That's absurd. There were miles of graves and the funerals were passing the hotel all day.'

'You were nowhere near them, I hope?'

She was alarmed, remembering the corpse she had viewed from the gharry: 'Why, are the bodies infectious?'

'I don't think so, but I don't know much about it. You'd better have a drink.'

With matter-of-fact kindliness, he gave her a half-tumbler of brandy which she gulped down. Becoming more cheerful, she said, 'If I have to die, I might as well die drunk.'

Dobson went out to the telephone. When he came back, he told her there was a taxi waiting for her at the door. He was sending her to the American Hospital for a check-up. He expected her to go at once and she did not blame him. The flat was an embassy flat and the last thing he wanted was to be responsible for spreading the epidemic in Cairo.

It was mid-day with the crowds pushing through the streets. On the bridge to Zamalek, she saw that soldiers were on duty directing people going east to walk on one pavement and the westward stream on the other. The taxi driver told her that this had been the king's own idea and was being enforced on his orders.

She thought, 'Silly, fat king.'

Coming in sight of the long, white hospital building, she felt she would be thankful to hand herself over to anyone who would accept responsibility for her tired and constantly ailing body.

10

The camp was on the move again. Allied forces had broken through the enemy front and Rommel was retreating.

Dawson told Simon: 'When we catch up with the old fox, we'll finish him for good and all.'

'It's been a great battle.'

'And a killing battle. The Jocks and the Aussies have had the worst of it.'

Simon told Dawson how one night, when he was lost among the forward troops, he heard bagpipes playing as a Scottish regiment advanced under enemy fire. He felt a catch in his throat as he remembered the thin wail of music but Dawson was not impressed.

'Foolhardy lot! That piper you heard was a boy with no more idea of modern warfare than his ancestors at Culloden. He walked at the head of the advance, unarmed, playing for dear life.'

'But did he get through?'

'Get through? Of course he didn't get through. He was down in the first ten minutes with his pipes dying out under him. A kid, a mere boy! His CO should've known better. Hopeless, these heroics!'

'Still, it was a pretty good show!'

'Good enough, but who paid the price? D'you know that one division reached Kidney Ridge led by a corporal? Every officer and NCO killed and no one left to lead except a ruddy corporal! But they got there.'

'Didn't the Jocks?'

'They got there all right, but not because they had a kid blowing bagpipes at the front.'

The forward troops advanced on Matruh and the camp followed them. Now there were only allied aircraft overhead, all travelling westwards to bomb the retreating enemy and the coast road jammed with Italian vehicles. Vast dust clouds on the horizon marked daily skirmishes but there was no major battle to finish Rommel 'for good and all'.

Simon asked, 'Where do you think the jerries are?'

Dawson could not say but it was his belief that 8th Army intended to cut the road ahead of the Afrika Korps. 'And then we'll have 'em all in the bag.'

Simon admired Dawson's prediction but nothing came of it. The Germans were retreating too rapidly to be overtaken and trapped.

Torrents of rain blotted out the ruins of Mersa Matruh and the yellow Matruh sand was spongy with yellow water. To make matters worse, the advance British tanks ran out of petrol and the reconnaissance planes reported: 'No sign of Rommel in the next eighty miles.'

Simon asked Dawson, 'Where do you think he's got to?'

'Seems like the desert fox has gone away.'

The rain stopped and the tarmac coast road gleamed and steamed in the afternoon sun. The sea, that had been leaden, regained colour and brilliance, and Simon, driving beside it, felt the excitement of the chase. During all his time in Egypt, the regions beyond the frontier had been enemy territory. Now he felt the whole of North Africa was opening to him.

The wire, great barbed rolls of it, put up by the Italians to keep the Senussi tribesmen out of Libya, was blasted with holes through which the allied armour and transports followed the defeated enemy out of Egypt. Simon, pursuing the pursuers, came to Sollum and Crosbie drove them up the escarpment through Halfaya Pass amidst a jam of military vehicles. This was the famous pass that the troops called Hellfire. The story was that a grounded airman was likely to be seized and held for ransom by the Bedu who would send his testicles to GHQ in proof of his sex and colour. Now it seemed petrol fumes rather than the risk of castration justified the nickname. At the top, they came on the white crenellated fortress of Capuzzo, much shot about, its ornamental gateway declaring itself to be: 'The Gateway of the Italian Army'.

The camp leaguered behind the mud-brick remains of Upper Sollum and Simon, with nothing to do till supper-time, walked down the escarpment to the lower village. From the distance, it looked a pretty place. A collection of small villas had been built on pink rocks beside a curving bay of pink sand. It was early evening and a mist, like fine powder, overhung the translucent green of the sea.

Coming down into it, he saw that the place was deserted and in ruins. The villas were collapsing into heaps of raw clay but plant life had sprung up after the rain. Bougainvillaea mantled the broken walls and the garden areas were furred over with new grass. During the five months' lull, while the contestants faced each other at Alamein, the splintered trees had regained them-selves and the bougainvillaea had flowered. In one pit, that had once held a house, poinsettias covered the ground so thickly, they formed a counterpane of scarlet lace.

The town was a small, seaside town and the fact made Simon think of Crosbie. He was beginning to like Crosbie better and had even learnt something about him. Crosbie's parents kept a shop in a small seaside town on the Lincolnshire coast. It was some time before Crosbie was brought to reveal that the shop was a fish shop and when the war started, he was just beginning to learn the trade.

'Did you like being a fishmonger?' Simon asked.

'Well, it's a job, isn't it?'

'You wouldn't rather do something else?'

'I did do something else. Sometimes, I drove the van.'

That, so far, was all Simon had learnt about Crosbie but it had roused his curiosity. Somewhere behind his blunt, blank face Crosbie had memories of another life lived before the war brought him here. In spite of his determination to avoid emotional relationships, Simon was becoming attached to Crosbie because, like Ridley, he felt the need for an attachment of some sort.

He wandered down to a small central square where a jacaranda, earliest of flowering trees, had covered itself with blue rosettes as though to hide its own desecration. He came to a café where a single chair had been left standing on a mosaic floor. The mosaic surprised him, then he realised this must have been an Italian town, an Italian seaside town.

He tried to imagine Ridley's small town shattered as this place was shattered, and he said to himself, 'Lord, the things we do to other people's countries!'

11

The American Hospital had one of the most pleasing aspects in Cairo. Harriet, put to bed in a white, air-conditioned room with a balcony, lay for a long time with her eyes shut, waiting for someone to come and investigate her condition. When no one came, she opened her eyes and staring out at the empty sky, she thought of her death in a foreign place. The poet Mangan had died of cholera and that death seemed nearer than all the deaths in Upper Egypt. Like Yakimov, who had died in Greece, she would be buried in dry, alien earth where her body would quickly turn to dust, and she would never see England again. The prospect did not greatly upset her, she felt too tired. She thought of Aidan crawling into the canvas shelter to die and could not see that she, herself, had much more reason to go on living.

She was roused by the Armenian nurse who told her in an awed whisper: 'Doctor come.'

The doctor was not, as she had expected, an American, but an Egyptian who spoke with an American accent. He announced himself: 'Shafik,' and bowed slightly.

'You have thrown up, yes?'

'No.'

'But your insides are upset? For how long?'

'A long time, on and off.'

'And now worse?'

'Yes.'

Dr Shafik examined her critically, without sympathy, almost

resentfully, as though annoyed that she should be there. She found his manner disconcerting and his appearance more disconcerting. Most Egyptians put on weight and looked middle-aged when they were thirty. Dr Shafik, who was thirty or more, had preserved his facial good looks as well as the slim elegance she had occasionally noted among young officers at the Officers' Club. He picked up her hand and examined it as though it were an entity all on its own.

'How much do you weigh?'

'Seven stone. That's one hundred pounds.'

'I think not. I think you weigh not even eighty pounds, but we shall see. One thing I can say: you haven't cholera.' He obviously thought her a fool for choosing such a sickness: 'There is no cholera in this part of Egypt.'

'I've just come from Upper Egypt where people are dying in hundreds.'

'Not of cholera. Malaria, more likely. Upper Egypt is malaria country.'

'Is there an epidemic form of malaria?'

Harriet's spirit broke the severe calm of Shafik's face. His long, firm mouth twitched slightly but he turned away before the twitch could become a smile. Leaving the room, he said, 'Tomorrow we will make tests, then we can see if you are ill or not.'

The possibility that she was not ill heartened Harriet and, seeing no reason to stay in bed, she rose, put on her dressing-gown and went out on to the balcony. The balcony overlooked the Gezira sports grounds. A grove of blue gums lined the hospital drive and looking down on them, she could see the crowns of blue-grey leaves moving and glittering in the wind. A couple of long cane chairs were on the balcony and sitting out in the brief splendour of the evening light, she was less inclined to contemplate death in Egypt. Instead she reflected on the recent news: the fact that Tobruk had been recaptured and Montgomery's claim that he had smashed the German and Italian armies, and she began to think of the war ending and a normal life beginning again. They could go back to England. With all that before her, why should she think of dying?

The crickets, brought out by the cooling air, were noisy in the grass below. As the sun sank, the different playing-fields – the polo ground, the golf course, the cricket field, the race course – merged into a greensward so spacious, it was like an English parkland. The club servants came out with lengths of hose and began to spray the grass with Nile water. As the light failed and mist rose from the ground, the white robes of the men glimmered through the twilight. The haze deepened over the acres of green but even when it had turned to dark, the servants were still visible, drifting about in their dilatory way, an assembly of shadows.

The nurse, who called herself Sister Metrebian, came looking for Harriet. Speaking in a small, gentle voice, she said, 'You should not be out here in the cold, Mrs Pringle,' but she left it for Harriet to decide whether she would go in or not. She was a yellow-skinned, plain, very thin, little woman with a solemn expression that, whatever her emotions might be, never altered. She simply stood and watched Harriet until Harriet rose from the chair and returned to bed. She was sitting up, her supper finished, when Guy entered amid his usual clutter of books and papers, and with his usual air of having made a temporary landing during a flight round the earth.

He kissed her, sat on the bed and said he could not stay long. Pushing his glasses up into his hair, he gazed quizzically at her and asked, 'What are you doing here? What's the matter?'

'I don't know, but it isn't cholera.'

'No one thought it was, did they?'

'Yes. Dobson couldn't get me out of the flat quickly enough.'

He shook his head, smiling with a frown between his brows. Worried by her loss of weight, he had wanted her to apply for a passage on the ship taking women and children to England, but that did not mean that, here and now, he could believe she was really ill.

'How long will they keep you here?'

'If there is nothing much wrong, I might be out tomorrow.'

This sensible reply cheered him and at once convinced that there was no cause for concern, he lifted her hand and said, 'Little monkey's paw! You won't be here long.'

That settled, he put aside the question of her health and talked of other things. It was not simply that he wished her to be well. Sickness of any sort was an embarrassment to him because he did not believe in it. Forced to accept that whether he believed or not, it existed, he saw it as a self-imposed condition, a mental aberration related to witchcraft, religion, belief in the supernatural and similar follies. So far as Harriet herself was concerned, he suspected a deep-seated discontent but as this could not relate to him or his behaviour, he preferred to forget about it.

'What happened in Luxor? Why did Angela come back so soon?'

Harriet told him of Angela's sudden anxiety and need to return and assure herself that Castlebar was alive and well.

'She's crazy,' Guy said. 'You do realise that, don't you? The woman's mad.'

Harriet laughed and went on to the subject of Aidan Pratt, describing their meeting and dinner at his hotel.

'He told me how he had been torpedoed in mid-Atlantic . . .'

'Yes, he told me, too. When we first met in Alexandria.'

So the confidence had not been, after all, a confidence. She could not doubt Aidan still suffered from the experience but she suspected that now he preserved his suffering and, relating it, felt himself enhanced by it.

She said, 'He tells it very well,' but Guy had lost interest in Aidan and would not discuss him or his misadventure.

'I've a lot on at the moment: not only the entertainment for the troops but Pinkrose's lecture is in the offing. He's fussing a lot. My idea had been a reasonably sized audience in the Institute hall but he thinks we should hire the ballroom at the Semiramis or the Continental-Savoy.'

Professor Lord Pinkrose had been sent out from England to give an important lecture in Bucharest but had arrived amidst political disorder so no lecture was possible. He had hoped to make up for this in Athens where there had been the same difficulty in finding a hall. In the end he had lectured at a garden luncheon given in Major Cookson's Phaleron villa. 'A glittering party', he had described it: 'A sumptuous affair'. He clearly expected the Cairo lecture to be something of the same sort.

Harriet laughed: 'Why not get the ambassador to lend the Embassy ballroom?'

'Yes, he thought of that, too, and made me speak to Dobson who said it's been shut up for the duration. Pinkrose says if I don't make it a big social occasion, he won't give the lecture. I've got to humour him because the university people are impressed by him. He's a bigger name than any of us realised.'

As Guy lifted his wrist to look at his watch, Harriet said, 'Don't go. When your evening begins, mine will end. So stay a little longer.'

Guy settled back on his chair but it was evident he would go soon. 'I've a rehearsal with Edwina this evening. I promised I'd pick her up.'

Remembering the interlude she had overheard that afternoon, Harriet said, 'I'm not sure she'll feel like going.'

'Yes, of course she will.' Guy spoke with easy certainty, having found that people usually did what he wanted them to do.

'I suppose you're right.'

She had seen that, caught in the radiance of his enthusiasm, everyone proved to be a player at heart. Everyone, that was, except Harriet. She had been cast for the main part in his first production but after a couple of rehearsals, he had put her out of it. He said she was too involved with him but the truth was, she suspected, he felt she was not impressed, as the others were, by his personal magnetism. She was inclined to be critical.

For her part, she not only resented the time spent on the productions but she dreaded their possible failure. He had managed well enough so far. In Bucharest he had drawn in the whole of the British colony: a ready-made audience. In Athens, where every serviceman was a hero, he had had almost too much help and support. But here, in this big heterogeneous and indifferent city, where the soldiers were provided for and entertained till they were tired of entertainment, who would care?

She made a last appeal to him: '*Must* you go on with this show? Haven't you enough to do?'

'I never have enough to do.' He jumped up, enlivened by the

thought of the evening ahead: 'You wouldn't want my energy to go to waste, would you?'

She saw that only his constant activity enabled him to live with himself and she felt helpless against it. She began to see their differences as irreconcilable. He was never ill and did not understand illness. She wanted a union of mutual devotion while he saw marriage merely as a frame to hold an indiscriminate medley of relationships that, as often as not, were too capacious to be contained. She sighed and closed her eyes and this gave him excuse to go.

'It won't hurt you to have a rest in bed. I expect you overdid it, sight-seeing in Luxor.'

As he was leaving, Sister Metrebian came in with sleeping-tablets for Harriet. The sight of her with her plain face, her small chocolate-brown eyes, her reticence and air of enclosed sadness, brought Guy to a stop.

She offered the tablets to Harriet who said she did not need them. Sister Metrebian gently persisted: 'I am sorry, but you must take them. Dr Shafik wants you to sleep very well so tomorrow you will be fresh for the tests.'

Feeling he must make a gesture towards the nurse, Guy said cheerfully: 'I can see the patient is in good hands,' and as he smiled admiringly on her, Sister Metrebian's sallow cheeks were tinged with pink. Although she was by nature quiet, conveying her requests by movements rather than words, she said when Guy had gone: 'What a nice man!'

Growing drowsy, Harriet, lying in darkness, drifted in memory till she seemed back again in the haunted strangeness of child-hood. She had had pneumonia when she was a little girl. At first it was thought to be merely influenza and she had been put to rest on the living-room sofa, facing the fire. She remembered how the fire and the fireplace and the clock above it and the ornaments had become insubstantial, as though made of some glowing, shifting, magical stuff that enhanced the luxury of lying there, wrapped in warmth and comfort, drifting in and out of consciousness.

Her mother, becoming anxious, had put a hand on her forehead and said to someone in the room, 'She has a fever.' That, too, was part of luxury for her mother was not given to tenderness. She sometimes said, as though describing a curious and interesting facet of herself: 'I don't like being touched. Even when the children put their arms round me, I don't really like it.'

But Harriet was different and as sleep came down on her, she told herself, 'I want more love than I am given – but where am I to find it?'

Her first visitor next morning was Angela who arrived with an arm full of tuberoses that scented the room. She asked with intense concern, 'What is it? What is the matter with you?'

'Apparently nothing serious.'

'Oh, Harriet, what a fool I was dashing back to Cairo and leaving you on your own.'

'I was all right. I met a friend and saw the sights. But what came of your dash? – did you find Bill alive?'

'Need you ask? I went to the Union and there he was: smirking, with his bloody Mona smirking at his side. I realised then he'd never leave her. He dare not. He hasn't the guts. Harriet! I've decided, I'm going on that boat for women and children. I may go to England, or I may get off at Cape Town, but whatever I do, I'm going.'

Harriet could not take this declaration seriously: 'You can't go. You couldn't leave me without a friend.'

'I *am* going. I've already applied for a passage. I have to get away from Bill and I won't get away unless I do something drastic. So, to hell with him and his God-awful wife. Let him sit there and smirk. I have my own life to lead and I intend to have a rattling good time.'

'If you go to England, you'll be conscripted.'

'Not me. I know what to do about that. When they call you up, you just say, "I'm a tart". Tarts are exempt (God knows why). They say, "Oh, come now, Lady Hooper, you don't want us to think you're a common prostitute, do you?" and you say, "Think what you like. That's what I am: a tart," and if you stick to it, there's not a thing they can do about it.'

'But you're not a tart. You couldn't keep it up.'

'I could and, if necessary, I shall.'

'So you really mean to go?' Harriet became dejected as she saw Angela lost to her. 'You've made me feel miserable.'

'Then come with me.'

Harriet smiled. 'Perhaps I will,' she said.

No one was in a hurry at the American Hospital. Once there, Harriet was expected to stay there and when she asked Sister Metrebian if she could soon go home, the nurse shook her head vaguely: 'How can I say? First, they must examine the specimens.'

'And when will we get the verdict?'

'Tomorrow, perhaps. The day after, perhaps.'

But the result of the tests was slow in coming and when Harriet enquired about it, Sister Metrebian became distressed: 'How can I say? You must wait for Dr Shafik.'

'When will he be back?'

Sister Metrebian shrugged: 'He is a busy man.'

That was not Harriet's impression of Dr Shafik. Sometimes, from boredom, she went out in her dressing-gown and wandered about the passages of the hospital, seeing no one and hearing nothing until, passing through a gate marked 'No Entry', she came into a cul-de-sac where there was only one door. Behind the door a man was shouting in delirium, expressing a terror that seemed to her more terrible because it was in a language she did not understand. As she hurried back to her own room, she met Sister Metrebian and asked her what was wrong with the man.

Sister Metrebian shook her head in sombre disapproval: 'You should not go near. He is very ill. He is a Polish officer from Haifa where they have plague.'

'*Plague*? He has got plague?'

'How can I say? He is not my patient. I can say only: you must not go near.'

Trembling, Harriet sat on her balcony, gulping in fresh air as though it were a prophylactic, and she thought of England where there was no plague, no cholera, no smallpox, and the food was not contaminated. If she went with Angela, she would regain her health – but how could she leave Guy here alone?

She had said to Angela, 'You know what happens when wives go home? We've seen it often enough.'

Angela took this lightly: 'You know you can trust Guy. He's not the sort to go off the rails.'

Perhaps not, but it was Guy who had first suggested she ask for a passage on the boat and she was suspicious of the fact he wanted her to go. She thought, 'Everything has gone wrong since we came here. The climate changed people: it preserved ancient remains but it disrupted the living. She had seen common-place English couples who, at home, would have tolerated each other for a lifetime, here turning into self-dramatising figures of tragedy, bored, lax, unmoral, complaining and, in the end, abandoning the partner in hand for another who was neither better nor worse than the first. Inconstancy was so much the rule among the British residents in Cairo, the place, she thought, was like a bureau of sexual exchange.

So, how could she be sure of Guy? When she married him, she scarcely knew him and, now, did she know him any better? How rash she had been, rushing into marriage, and how absurd to imagine it, on no evidence at all, a perfect, indestructible marriage! Every marriage was imperfect and the destroying agents, the imperfections, were there, unseen, from the start. How did she know that Guy, under the easy-going, well-disposed exterior, was not secretive and sly, suggesting she return to England for his own ends, whatever they might be?

It was noon, the most brilliant hour of the day, when the Gezira playing-fields looked as dry as the desert. The sky was colourless with heat yet to her it seemed to be netted over with darkness. The world seemed sinister and she felt she could put no trust into it. Aidan Pratt had said of life: 'If it has to end, does it matter when it ends?' The same could be said of life's relation-ships. If Guy were a deceiver, then the sooner she found out, the better.

Later that afternoon, when she had returned to bed, Dr Shafik entered with a springing step and, standing over her, looking satisfied with himself, he said, 'Well, madame, we have discovered your trouble. You have amoebic dysentery. Not good, no, but not so bad because there is a new drug for this condition. The American Embassy has sent it to us and you will be the first to benefit by it.'

'And I will be cured?'

'Why, certainly. Did you come here to die?' Tall and handsome in his white coat, Dr Shafik smiled an ironical smile: 'Could we let a member of your great empire die here, in our poor country?'

'A great many members of the empire are dying here. You forget there is a war on.'

Harriet could see from his face that Dr Shafik had forgotten but he hid his forgetfulness under a tone of teasing scorn: 'Call that a war? Two armies going backwards and forwards in the desert, chasing each other like fools!'

'It's a war for those who fight it. And may I ask, Dr Shafik, why you have to be so unpleasant to me?'

Surprised by the question, he stared at her then his smile became mischievous: 'Are you aware, Mrs Pringle, that we have here another English lady?'

'No.' Harriet had not heard of an Englishwoman being in hospital but there were a great many English people not known to her in Cairo. Some lived half-way between the Orient and the Occident, avoiding the temporary residents brought here by war. Some had adopted the Moslem religion and its ways. Some had married Egyptians and others, though they went to England to find marriage partners, had lived here so long, they had become a race on their own.

'Is she very ill?'

'She was, but now she is recovering. Would you wish her to come and talk to you?'

Harriet knew that he meant to play some trick on her but asked from curiosity, 'What is her name?'

Shafik was not telling: 'Perhaps when you see her, you will know who she is.'

He went, promising that the lady would visit her, and an hour later a very old woman came sidling into the room, wearing a hospital bath-robe and a pair of old camel-leather slippers that flapped from her heels. She crept towards the bed and Harriet, seeing who she was, said, 'Why, Miss Copeland, what are you doing here?'

She had last seen Miss Copeland in the pension where the Pringles lived before moving to Dobson's flat. She came in once a week to lay out a little shop of haberdashery which, to help her, the inmates bought, whether they needed the goods or not. She had not changed; her skin, stretched over frail, prominent bones, still had the milky blueness of extreme age. At some time during her long sojourn in Cairo, she had become deaf and had shut herself into silence, seldom speaking.

Though she knew the old woman could not hear her, Harriet said to encourage her: 'Why are you here? You look quite well.'

Miss Copeland sat on the edge of the chair. Her pale, milky eyes observed the things about her and when they came to Harriet, she whispered: 'They found me in bed. I couldn't get up.'

'What was the matter?'

'I was riddled with it.'

Much shocked, Harriet could think of nothing to say. Seeing that her lips did not move, Miss Copeland leant towards her and enquired: 'What did you die of?'

Before Harriet need answer, Miss Copeland jumped down from the chair: 'It must be time for lunch. It's nice being dead, they give you so much to eat.' She was gone in a moment, her slippers flapping behind her.

Almost at once, Dr Shafik came in to discover how Harriet had taken the visit: 'So, you have seen the lady? You know her, I think?'

'I know who she is. Has she really got cancer?'

'No. That is her little fantasy. But is she not charming? An old, harmless lady, living here among other ladies of her own country – and yet she nearly starved to death. She lay in bed, too ill to move, and no one called to see how she was. It was a poor shop-keeper, where she bought bread, who asked himself, "Where is the old English lady? Can she need help?" – and so she was found.'

Discomforted, as Dr Shafik intended her to be, Harriet said,

144

'We knew nothing about her. She made some money by selling little things: tapes, cottons, needles, things like that. She was independent. She lived her own life and did not seem to want anyone to call on her . . .' Harriet's defence faded out because, in fact, no one knew how or where Miss Copeland lived, and she wondered whether anyone cared.

Shafik nodded his understanding of the situation: 'So you left her alone and it was an Egyptian peasant who showed pity! You see, here in Egypt, we live together. We look after our old people.'

'Miss Copeland didn't want to live with anyone. She wanted to be alone so, when she needed help, there was no one at hand to give it.'

Shafik gave a scoffing laugh: 'Now you know she needs help, will you, with your large house and many servants, take her in?'

'I might, if I had a large house and servants, but I haven't. My husband and I have one room in someone else's flat.'

'Is that so?'

'You did not answer my question, Dr Shafik. I asked why you are so unpleasant to me?'

He again left the question unanswered but later in the day, when Edwina came to see her, she had an answer of sorts.

Edwina, her tear-reddened eyes hidden behind dark glasses, said, 'Oh, Harriet, I couldn't come before. I couldn't . . .' She put her head down and sobbed again and it was some minutes before she could continue: 'Peter's gone back to the desert. I'll never see him again . . . I'll never . . .'

'Don't worry, you will see him again. The next thing will be a counter-offensive and they'll all be belting back to Sollum and coming to Cairo on leave.'

'That's not what he thought. He said, "This time we've got them on the run."'

'They say that every time.'

Harriet brought out a bottle of whisky, given her by Angela, and said, 'Let's have a drink. It'll do us both good.' As Edwina sniffed and drank her whisky, Harriet said, 'Even if he doesn't come back, there are other men in the world.'

'That's true. Guy's been terribly kind to me.'

'He's kind to everyone,' said Harriet who had no intention of offering Guy as one of the 'other men'.

But Edwina was not to be discouraged: 'You know, I think Guy arranged this whole entertainment just to take my mind off Peter.'

'He arranged it long before Peter became troublesome.'

A number of people, Aidan Pratt among them, had imagined they were the sole recipients of Guy's regard. And yet . . . And yet . . . It was Edwina's singing voice that had induced him to plan a troops' entertainment.

Warned by Harriet's silence, Edwina said no more about Guy but diverted her by giggling: 'I see you've got that gorgeous Dr Shafik! How romantic, lying here pale and interesting, with Dr Shafik taking your pulse!'

'Amoebic dysentery is not a romantic condition.'

'*Condition du pays*. I bet he's had it himself.'

'And he's not gorgeous to me. He's downright disagreeable.'

'Oh, he's disagreeable to all of us. He's violently anti-British. He belongs to the Nationalist Party and that's worse than the Wafd. They'd cut our throats tomorrow if they had the chance.'

'Good heavens, Dr Shafik has every chance in the world here. I hope Sister Metrebian will protect me from him.'

Edwina, having finished her whisky, became wildly amused by this but her laughter changed in a moment and she choked with sobs: 'Oh, Peter, Peter, Peter! I long to have him back!' She was desolate but not to the point of admitting that Peter was married to someone else.

Harriet, knowing what she did know, said, hoping to pull her together, 'I'm sorry, Edwina dear, but I think you're well out of it. He'd make a terrible husband. All that fooling about! What a bore!'

'You're probably right. Yes, I know you're right. There were times when I could have murdered him. Although he's got a title, he's a brute, really.'

Edwina dabbed her eyes, then murmured, 'Still . . .'

A brute, but, still, no ordinary brute! He was a catch – alas, already caught! Edwina sighed. Her golden beauty drawn with disappointment, she saw herself setting out again to find another 'catch'. There were a great many lonely men in Cairo but few who matched up to Edwina's aspirations.

Her regimen of emetine capsules and a bland diet seemed so simple, Harriet thought she could treat herself at home but Sister Metrebian would not hear of it: 'We have to carefully watch you. Emetine is very dangerous. A toxic drug. You take too much and you kill yourself. Do you understand?'

And, Harriet thought, how easily Dr Shafik could kill her! When she had been in hospital a week, he entered the room in a businesslike way and said he needed a sample of her blood. Sister Metrebian was at his heels, carrying a knife in a kidney dish. He lifted the knife and Harriet was startled to see it was sharp-pointed like a kitchen knife.

'What is this?' he asked: 'We have here an edge like a consumptive's temperature chart!' He threw the knife back with elaborate disgust and she realised it had been another joke. He did not mean to use it, yet, in her distrust of everyone and everything, she felt a particular distrust of Shafik. She thought, 'The smiler with the knife', and asked: 'Why do you want a sample of blood?'

'For a little test, that is all. You are afraid?'

'No, of course not.'

She expected him to draw off the blood with a syringe but he had found another instrument which he wished to try. She felt he was experimenting on her. He pressed the point of a metal scoop into the artery of her inner arm. As the blood flowed down the scoop to a test-tube, she felt she could bear no more. Tears ran down her cheeks and Dr Shafik spoke with surprising kindliness: 'There, there, Mrs Pringle, don't cry. You are a very brave girl.'

Knowing she was not a brave girl, Harriet laughed but he did not laugh with her. The blood taken and the small wound covered, he pressed his long, strong fingers into the region round her liver and asked, 'Does that hurt?'

'Yes, but it would, anyway, you're pressing so hard. Why? What else is wrong with me?'

'That is a thing I must find out.'

When doctor and sister had gone, Harriet asked herself how it was she had sunk so low, she wept at the sight of her own blood? She despised herself and yet she wept again. Hunting round for a handkerchief, she found among the detritus at the bottom of her handbag, the heart made of rose-diamonds. She had forgotten it and now, holding it above her head, she was entranced by the radiance of the diamonds and was amazed that they were not merely in her keeping, like Aidan's votive cat, but were her property. The heart had been given to her: an object from a richer, grander, altogether more opulent world than any she had inhabited. She put it on the bedside table where it lit the air, a talisman and a preserver of life.

When Guy came in that evening, Dr Shafik was in the room, making a routine visit. He was about to rush away when it apparently occurred to him who Guy was. He came to a stop, held out his hand and said with awe: 'But, of course, you are the Professor Pringle that people speak of. You are a lover of Egypt, are you not? You are one who would urge us towards freedom and social responsibility?'

The revelation of his breadth of vision surprised even Guy but, pink with pleasure, he seized on Shafik's hand and admitted that he was indeed that Professor Pringle, saying, 'Yes, Egypt must have freedom. But social responsibility? That, I imagine, can come only through a Marxist revolution.'

Whether the doctor agreed or not, he moved closer to Guy and said in a quiet voice: 'You know, there are many of us?'

'Of course. I've talked to students . . .'

'Oh, students! They act and so are useful, but they do not think, and so are dangerous. But enough for now. We will talk another time, eh? Meanwhile, I have this case of your wife. She is not well.'

Guy, forced to revert to the discouraging subject of Harriet's health, asked: 'Aren't you satisfied with her progress?'

'Not so much. These amoebae are insidious animalcule. They move from organ to organ.'

Guy stared and kept quiet while the doctor, supposing the matter to be of intense interest to him, described the dangers of amoebic infection: dangers comprehensible by a male brain but not, of course, by a female.

'You must know that the amoebae can be carried in the portal stream to the liver and cause hepatitis and the liver abscess. If they reach the gall bladder that, too, can be bad. But I do not think she has the liver abscess.'

'Oh, good!' Guy, his dismay rapidly dispersed by this assurance, said, 'Then she's all right. There's nothing to worry about?'

'Sooner or later, she will be all right.'

'Splendid!' That decided, Guy was eager to return to the subject of social responsibility but Shafik seemed equally eager to evade it.

'Such talk would bore a lady, and you and your wife must have much to say to one another.' With an amused expression, lifting his hand in an adieu, the doctor made a swift departure.

Guy gazed regretfully after him: 'Why did he go off like that?'

'Sister Metrebian says he is a busy man.'

'I suppose he is.'

Now that the chance to discuss social responsibility had been snatched from him, Guy looked tired. He, too, was a busy man and he seemed to have about him the oppression of the dusty, noisy Cairo streets. He sat down and, as he looked at Harriet, she felt he reproached her for remaining in a country that was destroying her health.

'Dobson was telling me that before the war, anyone who contracted this sort of dysentery was shipped home. In England, the amoebae leave the system and you are not reinfected. Here, if you're prone to it, you're liable to get it again.'

'So Dobson wants to ship me home? He's absurdly selfimportant at times. He thinks he's only to say the word and I'll get straight on to the boat. Well, I won't. It would simply mean you were alone here and I would be alone in England. A miserable arrangement!'

'He's only thinking of your good. He says when people are depleted by acute dysentery, they pick up other diseases and . . .'

'And die? Well, let's wait till I show more signs of dying.'

He was about to say more when he noticed the rose-diamond brooch on the table beside her and he became animated: 'Where did you get this?'

'Angela gave it to me. She bought it in the Muski.'

He picked it up and laughed as he examined it: 'It's vulgar but it has a sort of panache. Let me have it. I'll give it to Edwina to cheer her up.'

'But it's mine. It was given to me.'

'Surely you don't want it. You couldn't be seen wearing a thing like that. It's a theatrical prop: just right for Edwina when she sings, "We'll meet again" or "Smoke gets in your eyes".'

'She doesn't sing those sort of songs.'

'She does in the show. It's for troops and the troops will love this thing.'

'It's a valuable piece of jewellery. They're real diamonds and cost a lot of money.'

'Even so, it's tawdry. It looks cheap.'

Smiling his contempt, he held the brooch away from him and she saw it degraded from a treasure and a talisman into a worth-less gewgaw. She could not defend it, yet she did not want to lose it.

She said, 'Give it back,' unable to believe he would take it from her, but he slipped it into his pocket.

'Darling, don't be silly. You know you don't want it. Let Edwina have it. Well, I must go.'

She watched, silent in disbelief, as he left with the brooch, delighted that he had something to give away.

'But what he gives, he takes from me!' She went to sit on the balcony, feeling, as the first shock of the incident wore off, a sense of outrage that the brooch was gone. Gazing over the greensward where she sometimes saw men on polo ponies and other men swinging golf clubs, she asked herself, 'What is there to keep me here?'

When Angela came to see her again, she said, 'I've been thinking about England. I could get a job there. I'd be of some use in the world.'

'Do you mean you might come with me?'

'Yes, I do mean that. I've been watching those men out there playing ridiculous games while other men are being killed, and I thought how futile our life is here. I felt I wanted to get away.'

'If you're serious, you'll have to apply at once. There's a rumour that the ship's over-full already. Shall I speak to Dobson? Get him to use his influence?'

'Yes, speak to Dobson.' But though she agreed, Harriet was still half-hoping that the ship was too full to take her and she would have to stay.

Still, she had put the matter into Angela's hands and before they could say anything more about it, she was visited by Major Cookson. He had not come alone. His companion, whose function had probably been to pay for the long taxi drive to the hospital, did not follow him to the bed but stood just inside the room as though bewildered at finding himself there.

Cookson sat on the bed edge and whispered to Harriet and Angela: 'I've brought an old friend, very distinguished. I knew you'd be pleased to meet him.' He turned and summoned the friend in a commanding tone: 'Humphrey, come over here.' Then returning to the women, he whispered again: 'It's Humphrey Taupin, the archaeologist. You were in Greece, Harriet. You must have heard of him.'

They all looked at Humphrey Taupin as he managed to make his way to the bedside where he stood, swaying, as though about to crumple to the floor.

Cookson brought a chair for him, saying, 'Sit down, Humphrey, do!' but Taupin remained on his feet, looking at Harriet, a smile reaching his face as though from a great distance.

Harriet had heard of him. He had been a famous name around the cafés in Athens. When he was very young, on his first dig, he had come upon a stone sarcophagus that contained a death-mask of beaten gold. The mask, thought to be of a king of Corinth, was in the museum and Harriet had seen it there. This find, that for some would have been the beginning, was for him the end. She could imagine that such an achievement at twenty might leave one wondering what to do for the next fifty years. Anyway, confounded by his own success, he had retired to the most remote of the Sporades; and no one had thought of him when the Germans came.

But he had escaped somehow and here he was, in Cairo, standing beside her bed. When she smiled back at him, he moved a little closer to her and a smell of the grave came from his clothes. His light alpaca suit hung on him as on a skeleton. He was in early middle-age but his hair was already white and his face was crumpled and coloured like the crust on old custard.

She asked him how he had escaped from Greece. When it occurred to him that she was speaking to him, he did not reply but bent towards her and offered her his hand. She took it but not willingly. She had heard that he had been cured of syphilis, but perhaps he was not cured. Feeling his hand in hers, dry and fragile, like the skeleton of a small bird, she remembered the courteous crusader who took the hand of a leper and became a leper himself. When Taupin's hand slipped away, she felt she, too, was at risk.

Cookson plucked at his jacket, telling him again to sit down but his senses seemed too distant to be contacted. He smiled then, turning, wandered back across the floor and out of the room.

Cookson tutted and said, 'He really is a most unaccountable fellow. I'm sorry. I thought he would amuse you.'

Harriet, still feeling on her palm the rasp of Humphrey Taupin's hand, asked, 'How did he get here?'

'He's just arrived from Turkey. His Greek boys managed to get him to Lesbos in a caique in the middle of the night. He went on to Istanbul and he hung around there till the Turks threw him out.'

'Why did they do that?'

'Hashish, y'know. They're sticky about that.'

Angela asked: 'Is that why he's so vague?'

'Oh, my dear, yes. I went to that island of his once. Quite an ordeal, getting there and even more of an ordeal staying there. He kept you sitting up, talking, all night and if you got any sleep, it was during the day. Only one meal was served and not very good either. He called it breakfast. It arrived about ten in the evening and then the talk began.'

'I suppose he was more *compos mentis* in those days?' Harriet asked.

'Much more. He was quite the tyrant before he got on to hashish. He had three subjects: sex, literature and religion. You discussed one a night and then you were told the boys would row you back to Skiros. There was no knowing how long you would have to wait for the boat back to Athens.'

'And that was the routine?'

'Yes. Invariable. Everyone who went, talked about it.'

'But they did go?'

'Yes. Out of curiosity, as much as anything. We formed quite a little élite, those of us who'd braved the island. We felt we'd done something remarkable.'

'Yet when the Germans were coming, you all forgot about him?'

'Oh!' Major Cookson's mouth fell open, then he tried to excuse himself: 'It was so sudden, the German breakthrough. They came so quickly.'

'Still, you had time to prepare your get-away.'

Major Cookson hung his head, knowing that the manner of his departure from Greece might be forgiven, but it would never be forgotten.

Having discovered that Harriet was the wife of a professor who was a lover of Egypt, Dr Shafik changed towards Harriet. Whenever he had nothing else to do, he would stroll into her room and entertain her with flippant and flirtatious talk. He did not suppose her capable of discussing an abstruse problem but he would gaze at her thoughtfully, even tenderly, and accord her his especial care. Harriet knew that Arabs, when not laughing at the female sex as a ridiculous aberration in nature, were romantic and generous, but she became bored by his levity. She broke into it to ask, 'Is your plague patient still alive?'

'Yes, he is alive. How did you know I have such a patient?'

'I heard him crying out in delirium. It was frightening. And he's still alive! Is there a new drug with which to treat bubonic plague?'

'Yes.' He was rather sulky at being forced into this conversation and she had to question him before he would tell her: 'There is a serum which is effective, sometimes. But his heart will be weak.'

'You are not afraid for yourself?'

'Naturally I have been inoculated. We wear special clothing and so on. The danger is not great.'

'The man is a Polish officer, isn't he? Why was he brought to a civilian hospital?'

'He had to be isolated, and the military have no suitable place. You know, on this spot, a long time ago, there was the old quarantine station and hospital. The island was only half formed then, and it was desert.'

Harriet's interest, arising out of her horror of contagion, led Shafik to talk in spite of himself. He told her it was there that patients were brought during the plague epidemic of 1836. 'There was a Dr Brulard. He wanted so much to know how plague was transmitted, he took the shirt from a dead man and wore it himself. Was he not brave?'

'My goodness, yes. And did he catch plague?'

'No, nor did he solve the mystery of how it was transmitted. And there was typhus – now, how did they catch typhus?'

Harriet laughed nervously and Shafik refused to tell her any more about plague and typhus, but, leaning towards her, he said, 'You are getting better. Are you glad you did not die and go to heaven?'

'I thought there was no heaven for women in your religion.'

'Wrong, madame, wrong. The ladies have a nice heaven of their own. They are without men but there is a consolation: they are beautiful for ever.'

'If there are no men, would it matter whether they were beautiful or not?'

'Ha!' Dr Shafik threw back his head and shouted with laughter: 'Mrs Pringle, I am much relieved. You are, after all, a true woman.'

'Why "after all"?'

'I wondered. I thought you were too clever for your sex.'

'And you're not as clever as you think you are.'

'Oh, oh, oh!' Shafik shook his hand as though it had been burnt: 'How ungrateful, after I have so cleverly cured you!'

'Perhaps you didn't cure me. Perhaps I cured myself. You see, I have given in. I'm going back to England.'

'You are going to England?' he stared with concern and dismay: 'Just when we have become friends! And Professor Pringle? – he, too, is going to England?'

'No. He has to stay here till the war ends.'

'But, does he want you to go?'

'He thinks I will never be well while I remain here.'

'I'm sorry you are going.'

'I'm sorry, too.'

Before she left the hospital, Harriet asked if she might see Miss Copeland again, but Miss Copeland was no longer there. When he suggested that the Pringles should give her a home, Dr Shafik had been making fun of Harriet. A home already had been provided by the Convent of the Holy Family and there Miss Copeland could stay for the rest of her life.

Shafik, saying goodbye to Harriet, held her hand between his two strong, slender hands and said, 'One day you will come back to Egypt and then you will come to see me. Yes?'

Harriet promised that she would. Looking into his large, dark, emotional eyes, she almost wished she had an Oriental husband, especially one who looked like Dr Shafik.

12

For a fortnight before the lecture, Pinkrose telephoned Guy several times a day, demanding to know what progress had been made in finding a hall that would reflect his importance. He rejected the assembly rooms of the American University, the cathedral, Cairo University and the Agricultural Museum. None of these were grand enough for the occasion he had in mind. He wanted a large and ornate hall, one suited for the entertainment of royalty and the Egyptian aristocracy.

Cairo offered nothing to suit him. The Egyptians themselves when gathering for a wedding or the funeral of a notable, employed a tent-maker to erect a tent in a Midan or some other open area. These tents, large, square and appliquéd all over with coloured designs, had appealed to Harriet and she suggested that one be hired for the lecture.

Pinkrose was appalled by the idea: 'Lecture in a tent, Pringle! Lecture in a tent! Certainly not. What do you think I am? – Barnum's Circus?' He insisted that the Embassy be again approached and asked to open up the ballroom.

To please him, Guy had another word with Dobson who only laughed: 'The place is under dust sheets. It would take an army of servants to get it ready.'

In the end, Guy approached the management of the Opera House and found it was available if the sum offered were large enough. But even the Opera House did not please Pinkrose. Forced to accept it, he frowned at the bare stage and said, 'I expect you to pretty it up, Pringle.'

'We'll surround the podium with flowers and ferns.'

'Fair enough, Pringle; see to that. Now, about the reception. You know I've invited the king and court? Well, we can't ask them to sit on kitchen chairs, can we?'

The reception was to be in the Green Room which looked well enough to Guy but did not satisfy Pinkrose who went off on his own and found a shop that hired out theatrical furniture. He chose crimson plush curtains with gilt tassels and a large gilt and plush-seated chair that looked like a throne. These, together with two dozen gilt reception chairs, were delivered to the Opera House. When the curtains were hung and the chairs crowded into the room, Pinkrose called Guy in to admire the effect: 'What do you think of it, eh, Pringle? What do you think of it?'

'I think it's tawdry and ridiculous.'

'No, Pringle, it's regal. His majesty will think he's in a corner of Abdin Palace.'

'You know we've had no acceptances from the palace?'

'Oh, they'll come. They'll come.'

Guy had promised to call for Harriet when she left hospital but was too busy. He telephoned her at the flat to excuse his defection: 'By the time this lecture's over, I'll be as loony as Pinkrose.'

Losing patience, Harriet said, 'Why do you pander to the old egoist? Who cares whether he lectures or not?'

'You'd be surprised. The whole university staff is coming. And you'll come, too, won't you?'

Still toxic from the drugs that had killed the amoebae, Harriet had been thinking of going to bed. Persuaded to dress and attend the reception, she asked Angela to go with her.

'Oh, no, darling, I can't bear lectures. I forget to listen and I start talking and people around get shirty . . .'

'Do come, Angela, we'll sit at the back and laugh.'

'No, darling, no.'

Angela was firm in her refusal and suspecting she had some other engagement, Harriet went to the Opera House alone.

The Green Room was filled with gilt chairs but the guests, edged in among them, were neither numerous nor very distinguished. Pinkrose, ignoring the university staff and the government officials, waited, in a state of peevish anxiety, for someone worthy of his attention. He was wearing an old, greenish dinner suit with a grey knitted shawl over his shoulders. Usually he kept the shawl up to his mouth but now he had pulled it down in readiness for a royal welcome and his lips opened and shut in agitation.

Guy came to say the lecture should begin. Pinkrose, refusing to listen, shook his head: 'You must telephone the king's chamber-lain, Pringle. I insist. I *insist*. Make it clear that this is no ordinary lecture. I'm not just a don, I'm a peer of the realm. The palace owes me the courtesy of royal patronage.'

Guy, mild in manner but determined, refused to telephone the palace while the guests listened, transfixed by Pinkrose's behaviour.

'If you don't ring the palace, I won't go on. I won't. I won't. I won't.'

'Very well, I'll give the lecture myself.'

Pinkrose did not reply but stared at his script which shook in his shaking hands. When Guy asked the guests to follow him into the theatre, Pinkrose made a rush and pushed ahead of him. Trotting at a furious pace, he went down the aisle and up some side steps to the stage. Guy was to take the chair but before he could reach it, Pinkrose had positioned himself at the forefront of the stage and although he was still shaking, he seemed about to speak. His mouth opened but no sound came out. An oval figure, narrow at the shoulders and broad at the hips, he stared at the audience, his eyes stony with contempt. A stage light, shining down on his dog-brown hair, lit the ring on which his hat usually fitted.

He took a step forward. He was about to begin but before he could say anything, there was a report and he stood, looking astonished, saying nothing. The noise had not been very great and some people, thinking he was waiting for silence, shusshed at each other. Then they saw that he had a hand pressed to his side and his body was slowly folding towards the floor. As he collapsed, Guy hurried to him and pulling the shawl away, revealed Pinkrose's dress shirt soaked in blood. There was hubbub in the auditorium.

Harriet, going towards the stage, saw Guy's face creased with amazed concern. An army doctor ran up the steps to join him. Guy shook his head and the doctor, putting an ear to Pinkrose's chest, said, 'He's dead.'

This statement reached the people in the front row and was quickly passed back. A crowd of students leapt up and began bawling in triumph. One of them shouted: 'So die all enemies of Egypt's freedom.' The others, excited by the possibility of a political demonstration, repeated this cry while more sober members of the audience began pushing their way out before trouble should begin.

Harriet, standing below the stage, felt someone touch her arm and, looking round, saw a young woman who said, 'Remember me?'

'Yes, you're Mortimer.'

'Tell me, why are they saying Lord Pinkrose was an enemy of Egyptian freedom?'

Harriet could only shake her head but the student nearest to her answered: 'Not Lord Pinkrose. Lord Pinkerton. Minister of State. Very bad man.'

Another corrected him: 'Not Minister of State. Minister of War.'

Harriet said, 'Pinkrose isn't any sort of minister. You've killed the wrong man.'

Taking this as an accusation, the students began a clamour of protest: 'We did not kill any man.' 'Who is wrong man?' 'What's it matter, all British lords bad men. All enemies of Egypt,' and having found an excuse for a riot, they began tugging at the theatre seats in an effort to get them away from the floor.

The stage was empty now. Guy and the doctor had carried Pinkrose into the wings. Mortimer, holding to Harriet's arm, said: 'You don't look well.'

'It's the shock, and I've just come out of hospital.'

'Better get away from this rampage. No knowing what they'll do next.' Capable and strong, Mortimer put her arms about Harriet and led her out to the street. They stood in the cool, night air, listening to the uproar inside the theatre and waiting for Guy to emerge. He did not come but the students, defeated by the clamped-down seats, came running out, bawling every and any political slogan that came into their heads. Two of the young men, recognising Harriet, stopped, becoming suddenly cautious and polite. She asked them if they knew who fired the shot.

Speaking together, showing now vehement disapproval of what had happened, they told her that Egyptians were good people: 'Believe me, Mrs Pringle, we do not kill. We talk but killing is not in our nature.'

'Then who do you think did it?'

They looked at each other, hesitant yet unable to keep their knowledge to themselves. One said, 'They are saying a gun was seen. They are saying that Mr Hertz and Mr Allain were beside the door. When the shot came, they at once went out.'

'But who fired the shot?'

'Ah, who can say?'

An ambulance pulled up at the kerb. The watchers became silent, waiting to see what would happen next. Men went inside with a stretcher and when they came out, Guy was walking in front of them. The body, even more protected in death than in life, was muffled up like a mummy with Pinkrose's old, brown, sweat-stained trilby lying, like a tribute, on the chest. The body was put into the ambulance and Guy got in with it. Harriet moved to speak to him but he was driven away.

'So that's that,' Mortimer said: 'I could do with a drink. How about you? Shepherd's is too crowded. Let's get a taxi and go to Groppi's.'

Harriet, exhausted, was happy to let Mortimer find a taxi and help her into it. They found Groppi's garden nearly empty. The Egyptians were nervous of the winter air at night and the staff officers were thinning out as the desert war moved westwards. Cairo was no longer a base town though the townspeople, especially those who lived off the army, daily expected the British back again.

The two women sat in a secluded corner and Mortimer, attentive and concerned for Harriet, recommended Cyprus

brandy as a restorative for them both. They talked about Pinkrose and the manner of his death.

'He was advertised as Professor Lord Pinkrose,' Mortimer said:
'What was he doing here? Was he sent out to do some sort of
undercover work?'

'I don't think so.' Harriet described Pinkrose's arrival to lecture
in Bucharest, his move to Athens and then on to Egypt: 'I don't
think he dabbled in anything. I imagine, like Polonius, he was
mistaken for his better. The students mentioned a Lord Pinkerton.
That may have been the one the assassins were after. But how was
it you were at the lecture?'

'Oh, I'm addicted to lectures. I was a student myself when war
broke out. I was at Lady Margaret Hall. Seeing that a Cam-
bridge professor was to talk on Eng. Lit., I thought, "This will be
quite like old times." I went in with some idea of taking notes.
Keeping in training, as it were. I'll go back to study when the
war's over. Strange to think of it, though.'

'Did you know that Angela and I are leaving Egypt? We've
got berths on the ship going round the Cape to England.'

'Really, you're going? Both of you. Soon there'll be no one left
here. You sound sad. Do you mind leaving?'

'I do, strangely enough. When I first came here, I hated the
place. Now I feel miserable about leaving it. And, of course,
I'm leaving Guy. I won't see him again till the war's over – that
is, if it ever is over.'

'If you feel like that, why are you going?'

'I don't know. Out of pique, as much as anything.' Harriet
told Mortimer how Guy had taken the rose-diamond brooch and
Mortimer shook with laughter.

'You couldn't go because of that. It's too silly.'

'Not as silly as you think. He took the brooch to give to a girl
who's had an unhappy love affair. He thought it would comfort
her.'

'But it's not serious? – with the girl, I mean?'

'Perhaps not – but that detonated my feelings. I wanted to
change my life and did not know how to do it. This will be a
change. We know nothing about war-time England. I want

to go back and see for myself. I want to be in the midst of it.'

Mortimer ordered more brandy and they drank sombrely, Mortimer despondent at the departure of Angela, and Harriet despondent at having to depart. Buttoning her cardigan against the wind that rustled the creepers and shook the coloured lights, Harriet pictured England as a cold and sunless place, no longer familiar to her and so far away, it had become an alien country.

Mortimer said, 'I'm off to Damascus tomorrow. We leave at first light.'

'And when do you get back?'

'We never know for sure. We thought, this time, we'd go as far north as Aleppo.'

'Aleppo!' Harriet's fancy expanded through the Levant and hovered over a vision of Aleppo. She had come so far and seen so little: and, in spite of Dr Shafik's entreaty, she was not likely to return. But it was too late for regrets. She finished her brandy and said she had better go home to bed.

Walking with her down to the river, Mortimer said, 'I suppose you haven't been told the sailing date?'

'No. That'll be kept dark, for security reasons. We'll just have to wait till we receive a summons.'

'You'll go from Suez, of course. When you hear, give me a ring. Angela has my number. Leave a message if I'm not there; I'll ring you back. We often take the lorry to Suez to pick up supplies so, if we can, we'll come and wave you both goodbye.'

13

The German rearguards fought a delaying action outside Gazala and Dawson said, 'I think we've got him now.' The British infantry broke through but Rommel had already gone.

Simon, sent forward to check fuel supplies, drove through the detritus of battle, seeing among the seaside rocks, a litter of rusting vehicles. On the other side of the road, where the desert ran towards Knightsbridge and Sidi Rezegh, the abandoned hardware dotted the sand like herds of grazing cattle. Except for an old Lysander that chugged, slow and harmless, like a big daddy-longlegs in the sky, the whole field of past battles was silent.

Simon was content as he drove with Crosbie who, sitting beside him, had for him the wordless but companionable presence of a cat or dog. The familiar ordinariness of Crosbie was a comfort as the camp moved again and again, following the action as it went westwards into country Simon did not know.

On this quiet coast, with the sea lapping at their elbow, it seemed the war was as good as over. He said, 'We might be home for Christmas. D'you want to go back to fishmongering?'

'Don't know that I do,' Crosbie said.

Thinking of his return to a wife he had almost forgotten, Simon wondered how he would fit into a world without war. He would have to begin again, decide on an occupation, accept responsibility for his own actions. What on earth would he do for a living? He had been trained for nothing but war.

Outside Gazala, near the remains of a walled house, a tall palm marked the site of a water-tank. The palm attracted him, though he did not know why. Then he remembered the single palm he had seen and pitied in Cairo. This similar palm, swaying in the wind, was like something known and loved.

'A good place to eat our grub,' he said.

'Stop here, sir?'

'Yes. Get into the shade.'

As Crosbie ran the jeep under the palm, the ground rose about them and he rose with it. Simon, watching Crosbie's grotesque ascent, scarcely heard the explosion. He shouted, 'Bloody booby trap!' expecting Crosbie to shout back, then he was struck himself. Part of the mine's metal casing cut across his side and he was flung from the jeep.

This, he thought, was death, but it was not his death. Dragging himself round the jeep, seeing Crosbie sprawled a dozen yards away, he called to him: 'Crosbie. Hey, Crosbie!' but the man's loose straggle of limbs remained inert.

Simon tried to lift himself, with some idea of dragging Crosbie into the shade, but the lower part of his body would not move. And there was no shade. The palm, cracked through the stem, had broken in half and its fine head of plumes hung like a dead chicken. The jeep, too, was smashed and Simon's first thought was, 'How are we going to get back?' Oddly detached from his condition, he put his hand to his side and felt the wet warmth of blood. He said to himself, as though to another person: 'You were afraid to die like Hugo, and now this is it!' For some minutes death seemed like a fantasy then he realised it could be a reality. The action had moved so far forward, he was very likely to bleed to death before help came.

Putting his head in his hands, waiting for unconsciousness, he heard the sound of a vehicle and looked up. A Bren was lumber-ing and swaying out of the rubble, having collected the Gazala wounded, and he watched with little more than curiosity as it stopped beside Crosbie. Closing his eyes again, he heard a voice coming as from the other side of sleep: 'Let's take a shufti at that one over there.'

As they were lifting him into the Bren, Simon whispered, 'Never thought you'd come in time.'

The driver laughed good humouredly: 'Oh, we like to be in time, sir. That's our job.'

Inside the Bren with the wounded, Simon called out: 'What about my driver?'

'That chap over there? Mungaree for the kites, that one.'

'Can't we take him?'

'No, sir, can't take him. Got to get you and the others back to the dressing station.'

The Bren started up. Propped on his elbow, Simon stared out through the open flap at Crosbie's body till it became no more than a spot on the sand and then was lost to sight.

14

Only the English language papers reported the murder of Pinkrose. The *Egyptian Mail*, reputedly pro-British, published a leader entitled 'A Mystery'. Who, the editor asked, would wish to kill this great and good lord who was giving his lecture 'free and for no payment but love of his *confrères*?'

'Who, indeed?' asked Dobson when he read the article at the breakfast table, and he turned on Guy with an expression of ironical enquiry.

Everyone now knew that Hertz and Allain had left the Opera House immediately after the shooting and had not been seen since.

Guy, seldom confused, was confused now. He could not believe that Hertz and Allain were guilty; he could not believe that anyone was guilty, yet he could not deny that someone had killed Pinkrose. He could only say that Hertz and Allain were the two best teachers he had ever employed.

'And, anyway, it was a mistake,' Harriet said: 'The students were talking about a British minister with a similar name.'

Dobson sniffed, trying to contain his laughter: 'Is there a minister with a similar name? I don't think so. But a fellow did pass through Cairo a few days ago, on his way to Palestine. He was called Pinkerton.'

'Yes, the students mentioned Pinkerton. Who was he?'

'I can't say. Something very hush-hush, apparently. He said he was an official in the Ministry of Food. The only thing the British have to eat in Palestine are sausages, made by an English grocery shop called Spinney's. Very good they are. But this chap has been sent out to teach Mr Spinney how to make them out of bread instead of meat. To think of it! Poor old gourmandising Pinkers bumped off in place of a sausage-maker.'

Disliking Dobson's jocosity, Guy asked: 'Why should anyone want to murder a sausage-maker?'

'Who knows? Perhaps he wasn't a sausage-maker. He may have been an MI6 man in disguise.

'This is all nonsense. I don't believe Pinkrose was mistaken for anyone. He was on the platform, a target, and some fellow with a gun couldn't resist taking a pot at him.'

Dobson, becoming serious, nodded agreement: 'That's possible. Now the heat's off here, all the killers will be coming out of their holes.'

Guy and Major Cookson were the only people to follow Pinkrose's coffin to the English cemetery and neither could be described as a mourner. Guy went from a sense of duty and Cookson because he had known Pinkrose in better days. For Cookson even the dull ride into the desert outside Mahdi was a diversion. Coming back together into Cairo, Guy, who could not maintain enmity for long, decided that the major was not, after all, a bad fellow and stood him several drinks.

Harriet, thinking she might have died herself, asked what the English cemetery was like.

Guy said, 'A dreary place behind a heap of rubble. Poor old Pinkrose, with all his pretensions, would have demanded something better.'

In mid-December, the prospective passengers were informed that the ship – it was still known merely as 'the ship' – would sail early in January. English women and children from neighbouring countries began to congregate in Cairo, awaiting the exact date which would be announced twenty-four hours before the sailing.

A diplomat called Dixon wrote from Baghdad, asking Dobson to put his wife up during this waiting period. The flat being an Embassy flat, Dobson felt bound to comply and it so happened that a room was temporarily vacant. Its occupant, Percy Gibbon, had been sent on loan to the 'secret' radio station at Sharq al Adna, so Dobson wrote back saying he would welcome Mrs Dixon as his guest.

Without further notice, Mrs Dixon arrived as Hassan was setting the breakfast table. Six months pregnant, with a year-old son, a folding perambulator, a high chair, a tricycle, a rocking-horse and ten pieces of luggage, she stumbled into the living-room, exhausted by a long train journey, and sank on to the sofa. Dobson, called to attend her, went to look at Percy's room. It was only then that he realised it was locked and there was no spare key. He was ordering Hassan to go out and find a locksmith when Percy Gibbon let himself in through the front door. Percy stopped in the living-room to stare at the strange woman and her impedimenta then, sniffing his disgust, went to his room, unlocked it and shut himself inside it.

Hurrying from his room, Dobson said, 'Good God, who was that?'

Guy, who had seated himself beside Mrs Dixon in an attempt to cheer and comfort her, told him: 'It was Percy Gibbon.'

Dobson stood for a moment in helpless perplexity, then beckoned Guy into the bedroom. He whispered, 'You know, this is very awkward for me. I agreed to put her up, but where can I put her? Her husband's a colleague, so I can't tell her to go, but you, my dear chap, with your charm – you could, in the nicest possible way, of course, explain things to her. Tell her she'll have to find a room in an hotel.'

Guy was aghast at this request: 'I couldn't possibly. I've been talking to her, saying how pleased we all are to have her here. It would be such a shock for her if I told her to go. You see, everyone likes me. I'm not the person to do it. Ask Harriet. She's better at things like that.'

Harriet, appealed to, came from her room, thinking she could deal with the situation. Then she saw Mrs Dixon. Limp and near tears, trying to soothe her fretful child, she was a frail, little woman, her thin arms and legs incongruously burdened with her heavy belly, her fair prettiness fading, her apprehensions heightened by the awful appearance of Percy Gibbon.

She gazed at Harriet with anxious eyes and Harriet, saying

'Don't worry. We'll manage somehow,' went to speak to Dobson. 'Someone has to be sacrificed and it must be Percy Gibbon. Your room is big enough for two. You'll have to get a camp‚bed in here and share with him.'

'Oh, dear God, no! I couldn't bear it. And how could I persuade him to give up his room?'

'It's your flat. Don't persuade him, order him.'

Dobson again appealed to Guy: 'Come with me and help me to deal with Percy,' but Guy was in a hurry to get away. Agitatedly rubbing his soft puffs of hair, Dobson went to speak to Percy.

Hearing uproar from the bedroom passage, Mrs Dixon sat up in alarm then turned piteously to Harriet: 'Oh, this is my fault. I must go. We're not so poor we can't afford a room at Shepeard's.' She began gathering up the child and its belongings and Harriet had to explain that it was not a question of what one could afford. In Cairo, the few main hotels were so full that even senior officers had to share rooms and sometimes share beds. As for inferior hotels, she would find them intolerable.

Mrs Dixon remained on the sofa, watching fearfully as Percy passed through, carrying his belongings to Dobson's room. He looked blackly at her, muttering his rage as he went. His room vacated, Harriet went to look at it. It was the only one on the right of the corridor and it faced the blank wall of a neighbouring house. She now understood why Dobson had allowed Percy to remain in it. Who else would want it?

She said to Mrs Dixon, 'I'm afraid it's not much of a room.'

Lifting a hand, Mrs Dixon said, 'What does it matter? Anything will do.'

After Harriet had helped her unpack her immediate necessities, she dropped on to the bed and cried, 'Oh, to be safely on board ship.'

'Well, we will be soon, Mrs Dixon. But, meanwhile, you'll find the flat isn't so bad.'

Mrs Dixon smiled weakly: 'My name's Marion,' she said.

Marion Dixon, though grateful for Harriet's support, was chiefly admiring of Angela. Of the three women, united by the prospect of their long sea voyage, Angela was the most expectant of pleasure. Her hopes animated Marion and persuaded her that they were in for what Angela called 'a rattling good time'.

Angela, herself, having heard that many things in England were in short supply, spent much of the day shopping, coming back with parcels that she opened to amuse Marion. Marion had few interests, apart from the boy Richard, but she loved clothes and fingering Angela's silks and new dresses, she said, 'I long to get my figure back so I can wear things like that.'

While Edwina and the men were leaving for work, the three women lingered on at the breakfast table, suspended in the nullity of the present but promised a future of stimulating newness.

Angela often said, '*Bokra fil mish-mish.*'

First hearing it, Marion, who spoke a different Arabic, asked: 'What does that mean?'

'Apricots tomorrow: good times to come.'

Marion smiled her wan smile: 'I was so frightened but I'm not any more,' and she told her new friends that if, by some mischance, her baby was born at sea, their presence would console her.

Dobson laughed at them: 'You three, really! You're like a cluster of schoolgirls discovering sex.'

Edwina, feeling left-out, said, 'I wish I could go with you. But, of course, I can't. There's the show and I couldn't let Guy down.'

Harriet, putting her on trust, said, 'You'll look after Guy for me, won't you?'

'Oh, darling, you know I will. I'll see he doesn't get into mischief. You can rely on me.'

When the others had gone, the three sat in the darkened living-room where, even in winter, the shutters were put up against the sun that splintered in through the cracks. Some previous resident had had a fireplace built into a corner, a very inadequate fireplace. The only fuel to be found was cow-cake, which gave off more smoke than heat. The curious, bland smell of the smoke filled the flat and seemed to Harriet a part of the futility of her life in

Cairo. She told herself she was thankful to be leaving it and yet, at times, she was furious because she had agreed to go. It had all been decided too quickly. She should have dwelt upon it. She should have taken time to think. And now it was too late and she thought, 'At least, I'm getting away from this bloody show. I needn't care whether it fails or not.'

In her bleakest moods, she wondered what would happen to her in London. Angela talked as though their friendship would survive the displacement but Harriet realised, if Angela did not, that their social spheres were very different. Angela, who was wealthy, had wealthy friends. She jokingly spoke of them as the 'Q and G', the Quality and Gentry, and said they were brilliantly entertaining. 'You'll love them,' she told Harriet, but Harriet would have to work, not only as a reason for living. She would need the money. Guy could make her only a small allowance.

When she mentioned this to Angela, Angela said, 'I intend to work, too. I shall start painting again. You know, when he was killed, I was painting. That's why I didn't see what he had picked up. I thought I would never paint again, but it will be different in England. A new life, a fresh start. We'll find a flat with a studio. I'm told everyone's left London so you can get flats and studios for the asking.'

Harriet, sharing Marion's faith in Angela, said, 'Then we'll both work. Something to do: that's the most important thing in life.'

Flaunting her emotional independence, Angela said one evening, 'Let's go to the Union.'

'But Bill and Mona will probably be there.'

'What if they are? All that's in the past now. I'm indifferent to Bill. Let's go and say goodbye to the Union and thanks for the fun we had there.'

Marion refused an invitation to accompany them. Guy and Edwina were at a rehearsal, Dobson was out and having heard stories of children being raped by frustrated servants, she would not leave Richard alone with the safragis.

At the Union, Angela gave her usual order for a bottle of whisky and several glasses. Smiling mischievously, she said to Harriet, 'Let's see who we can pick up.'

They were soon joined by Jackman who seated himself as a right: 'Haven't seen you for ages. Not surprised. That rhinoceros, Bill's wife, would drive anyone away.'

'I don't see her here tonight.'

'No, Guy's talked her into that show of his. She's rehearsing, I believe.'

'And Bill? What's he up to?'

'Oh, he's around. I'm inclined to keep clear when he has Mrs C in tow.'

Hearing that Castlebar was alone in the club, Angela became silent and did not move till some instinct told her he was nearby. He came with his usual tentative, wavering walk and paused a few yards away. She slid her eyes to one side, observed him, then gave her whole attention to Jackman. He had been telling the women that in his opinion the 'Alamein business' had been a 'put up job': 'The order was "stretch them to breaking point" and they stretched them.'

Angela laughed flirtatiously at him: 'Come off it, Jake. You're a terrible liar. I never believe a word you say.'

Jackman, who had not noticed Castlebar, went on protesting his 'inside information' while Castlebar stood twitching and shivering like a hungry pariah dog that longs for sustenance but dares not approach too near. Angela, pretending to be absorbed by Jackman, again gave him an oblique glance and aware she was aware, he edged nearer and put his long, yellow hands together as though in prayer. Angela spoke sternly to him: 'Bill, come here at once.'

He advanced eagerly, his hands still held up, and muttered: '*Mea culpa. Mea maxima culpa.*'

'I agree. Sit down beside me. I require, as a penance, that you drink a very large whisky.'

Grinning delightedly, Castlebar sat where he was told while Jackman, realising he had been fooled, frowned and indignantly asked: 'Where did you come from?'

While Castlebar was setting up his cigarettes, Harriet said, 'So Mona is singing in the show? How did Guy manage that?'

Castlebar snuffled and giggled and said, 'You know what

your old man s like. He buttered her up till he had her eating out of his hand.'

When, Harriet wondered, did all this happen? – and where? She had the despairing sense of being completely outside Guy's life and she thought, 'At least I'm going in good time. I'm young enough to start another life.'

Angela, having permitted Castlebar to return to the circle, kept her head turned from him while he watched her, willing her to look at him. At last, forced to look round, she met his eyes and for a long minute they gazed at each other in meaningful intimacy, then Angela stood up. She said to Harriet, 'I think we should go.'

Flustered and disappointed, Castlebar wailed, 'You going already? The bottle's only half empty.'

'I'll leave it for you and Jake. We girls need our beauty sleep. I suppose you know we're going on the boat to England. We'll be away in a few days.'

Castlebar's mouth opened with shock and his cigarette fell between his knees. While he was scrabbling for it, Angela gripped Harriet by the arm and hurried her out to the gate where a taxi had just put down a fare. The two women got into it and, all in an instant, they were away.

'I thought you and Bill were about to be reconciled.'

Angela laughed: 'Never in this world. He won't have the chance to ditch me again. I said I was going and, I'm going. Tomorrow to fresh woods and pastures new.'

'You're very wise,' Harriet said, thinking that Angela was a great deal wiser than she expected her to be.

Dobson told the waiting women that, as another security measure, the ship might leave earlier than intended. He guessed the sailing date as 28 December.

With time so short, Harriet suggested to Angela that they visit the places they had always meant to visit. They should see the great mosques, the Khalifa and the zoo.

'Oh, what fun, yes,' Angela agreed, having the ability to find fun in everything. But next morning, when they were setting out for the zoo, the telephone rang. The call was for Angela who stood so long in the hall, talking in a low voice to the caller, she lost all interest in the zoo.

Coming back to Harriet, she said, 'I'm sorry, darling, but I don't think I can "zoo" it today. I've still so much shopping to do.'

'Shall I come with you?'

Angela ignored the question. Wherever she was going, she meant to go alone. A taxi was waiting for them and she said in agitated apology: 'You don't mind if I take it? Hassan can get you another one.'

Not waiting for an answer, Angela hurried from the flat and Harriet, at a loss, telephoned Mortimer to tell her their probable departure date.

'So you're really going? It sounds a bit mad to me,' Mortimer said.

'It is mad, but it's a solution, I can't go on living in limbo.'

'Well, if it's at all possible, we'll be there to see you off.'

It seemed then that everything was settled and, forgetting the zoo, Harriet went out to do some shopping on her own. Returning for luncheon, she found Marion in the sitting-room, gazing dully at Richard who was whimpering and throwing his toys about.

'Angela not back yet?'

Marion shook her head and Harriet asked, 'What have you been doing all morning?'

'Nothing. Richard's got nettle-rash. It makes him so cross, poor little fellow. Oh, Harriet, to be in England!'

England, it seemed, was a solution for every difficulty met here.

When Angela had not returned by tea-time, Harriet went to her room and was relieved to see her splendid cases still piled against the wall. Without reason, she had feared Angela had gone for good. Reassured, she told Hassan to bring in the tea-tray.

When he put down the tray, he said, 'Man here' and he handed Harriet a grimy slip of paper. It authorised the bearer to collect Lady Hooper's luggage. Going back to the room, Harriet

174

opened the wardrobe and found it empty. At some recent time, Angela had packed her clothes in expectation – of what? – perhaps only of a sudden summons to the boat.

The man stood humbly in the doorway and Harriet asked him: 'Where is Lady Hooper?'

He was one of the itinerant porters who sat about in the bazaars ready to transport furniture and heavy objects to any part of the city. He said, 'Lady say she send letter.'

'But where are you taking her luggage?'

'Lady say no say.'

Harriet motioned him to the cases. He was naked to the waist, short, square and strong-smelling. He belonged to the strict Moslem sect that believes the Messiah will be born of a male and he wore baggy pantaloons in order to catch the babe should it present itself without warning. He was dark-skinned but not negroid. The rope of his trade, his greatest and perhaps his only possession apart from the pantaloons, encircled his neck and massive shoulders. His air was savage but his manners were gentle and looking over the cases to compute their number, he touched them with an amiable, almost loving, respect. He regretfully shook his head. He could not carry them all at one time but would have to make two journeys. He asked would the lady be willing to pay so much? Harriet said she was sure she would.

He sorted the luggage into two heaps then, grunting and muttering instructions to himself, he roped cases on to his chest, back and sides, and hoisted others up to his shoulders.

Laden like a pack mule, he grunted his way out of the flat, leaving behind him a stench of stale sweat. Harriet threw open the verandah doors and went out into the fresh air. Looking down at him as he went among the poinsettias to the front gate, she saw that from bearing so much weight, his feet had become almost circular and appeared to have toes all round. She watched until he reached the road where he set off at a fast trot and turned the corner out of sight.

An hour passed, then he came back with the promised letter: 'Harriet, darling, you can guess what has happened. Bill has escaped but he's terrified she'll track him down. So we're going into hiding until she gets used to the separation. If she comes howling to you, tell her nothing. Sorry to miss the good times on board ship but you and Marion have fun for me. See you again one day. Love, Angela.'

'What good times, what fun?' Harriet asked aloud, angry that she had not foreseen what had happened. Angela had said she would not give Castlebar a second chance but Harriet, abandoned once, had not had the sense to see that the same thing could happen again.

No other word came from Angela. Rumours went round Cairo that she and Castlebar had been sighted in Jerusalem, in Haifa, in Tel Aviv and in Upper Egypt but their disappearance remained as much a mystery as the killing of Pinkrose.

Mona Castlebar did call at the flat, not 'howling' but in such fury, she could scarcely get a word out of her clenched face. When she found her voice, she accused Harriet: 'You know where they are, don't you?'

'No. Nobody knows.'

'My God, I'll do for them, you wait and see if I don't. He'll lose his job. He'll have nothing to live on. I hope they starve.'

'No danger of that. Angela has more than enough for both of them.'

'So that's it? She bought him with her money? I thought there must be something. He wouldn't have gone otherwise. She *bought* him.' Bitterly satisfied by this explanation of her husband's perfidy, she sat brooding on it as though she had nowhere else to go.

It was Christmas Day and everyone except Percy Gibbon had given presents to Richard. They littered the floor, to the annoyance of Percy who would, if he dared, have kicked them out of the way.

Mona watched Richard pushing the wheeled toys about then overturning them pettishly and whimpering his discontent. She looked as though she liked the scene no better than Percy did and at last, rising, she said, 'Well, there are some things to be thankful for,' and she took herself off.

Everyone was home for Christmas luncheon which was no different from any other luncheon. Richard, put into his high chair, struggled and cried and spewed out the soft-boiled egg which his mother tried to spoon into him.

Percy had seen this exhibition often enough but now, irritated by the toys on the floor, he stared at it with incredulous distaste so Marion became more nervous than usual. Her hand shook and the egg yolk went over Richard's chin and bib.

'Disgusting!' Percy said with feeling and Dobson remonstrated with him:

'Really, Percy, the child has to be fed.'

Brought to the point of open complaint, Percy hit the table: 'He needn't be fed in public. She could take him into her room – *my* room, I should say.'

Guy tried to reason with him: 'Oh, come now, Percy, the child has to be with adults in order to learn table-manners.'

Percy leapt up: 'Well, he won't learn them from me.'

'That's only too evident,' Harriet said.

At this, Percy strode into the room he shared with Dobson, slamming the door so violently, Richard began to scream and Marion to weep, asking: 'What am I going to do? What am I going to do?'

Harriet said: 'Put him in his pram and we'll take him to the zoo,' but Marion could not face the excursion. Weary of the petulant child, Harriet went to the zoo alone.

She walked across the river among crowds to whom Christmas Day, under the brilliant sky, was no better and no worse than any other day.

Just inside the zoo gates were the parrot stands, a long row of gaudy colours, each bird different from its neighbours. They gave occasional squawks but were too busy with preening and fussing and fluttering over their feathers to make much noise.

Harriet wandered round, desolate that, leaving Egypt, Angela was not going with her. There was no reason now for going at all. She had said to Dobson a few days before: 'I know you were kind, getting me a berth on the ship, but would it make any difference if I changed my mind?'

177

Dobson observed her reflectively: 'It would make a difference to you. You look as though a puff of wind would carry you away. You might catch anything in this condition. I recently heard of a chap who got tertian malaria and was gone in a matter of hours.'

And Harriet had taken on the responsibility of Marion who had been dismayed by Angela's flight and, in near panic, all her incipient apprehensions aroused, had said to Harriet, 'But *you* are coming, aren't you? You won't leave me. I don't know what I'd do if I lost you both.'

'Yes, of course I'm coming,' Harriet said and sighed.

She wondered now how long Marion would require her support. Angela had planned a life for herself and Harriet but neither thought to ask what Marion would do in England. Harriet, who often heard Marion sobbing behind the closed door of her room, had decided to find out.

She asked her, 'When you get to England, where will you go?' and was dismayed when Marion, her voice breaking, replied, 'I don't know.' She told Harriet that her parents were in India and her husband was expecting her to stay with his mother: 'But I know she doesn't want me. She's only got a small flat and there'll be nowhere for Richard to play. I keep asking myself, "Where will I go?" and I don't know. I don't know.'

'Why are you going at all?'

'It was Jim's idea. Richard's always unwell in Iraq and he gets on Jim's nerves. The truth is, Jim *wanted* me to go.'

This confession had a fatal ring for Harriet who, remembering it as she walked round the paths among the captive animals, thought, 'They want to get rid of us.' The friend who had made all possible, had deserted her. Left with an ailing woman, a complete stranger, who clung to her simply because there was no one else, she wondered, 'What on earth will I do with Marion all the way round the Cape and perhaps in England as well?'

She paused before one cage and another. The animals, comatose in the afternoon heat, seemed content enough. Then she came to a polar bear and stopped, appalled at finding an arctic animal in this climate. The bear was in a circular cage, not very big, an island of concrete surrounded by bars that rose up to a central dome from which water trickled constantly. The bear, sitting motionless under the stream, hung its head, torpid in its heavy white coat. Harriet felt it was in despair and leaning towards it, she whispered, 'Bear,' but it did not move. She was about to move on but, unwilling to leave the creature unaided, she went closer to the cage and stood for a long time, trying to contact the animal's senses through the medium of her intense pity for it. It did not move. She knew she could not stand there for ever but before she went, she said aloud, 'If I could do anything for you, I would do it with my whole heart. But the world is against us. All I can do, is go away.'

As Dobson had predicted, word came that the ship would sail on 28 December. The passengers were to board the boat train for Suez at ten a.m. on the sailing date.

'I'm sure you're thankful,' Guy said: 'You must be tired of all this hanging about.'

'I'm tired of the whole situation, but it's too late to argue about it. I suppose you'll come with me to Suez?'

'Come to Suez?' Guy was abashed by the very suggestion: 'How could I possibly come to Suez? You know the show is on New Year's Eve, and I'll be rehearsing day and night till it goes on.'

Harriet, expecting no other reply, was not even disappointed by it but said, 'The train is at ten a.m. tomorrow. I suppose you *will* come to the station to see me off?'

'Of course.' Guy, stung by the ironical inexpectancy of Harriet's tone, became apologetic: 'I'm sorry I can't come to Suez, darling. It never entered my head you would want me to, but I will be at the station. I'll dash into the office first thing then, when I've looked through my letters, I'll go straight to the station. I'll get there before you arrive.'

Next morning, left alone in the flat, Harriet and Marion sat in the living-room, waiting to depart. The flat was silent; even

Richard, tensed by the unusual atmosphere, had ceased to cry. Hassan had been sent out to find two taxis, the extra one to take the excess luggage.

The others had said their goodbyes after breakfast. Edwina, flinging her arms round Harriet, burst into tears: 'What shall I do without you?' and Harriet, remembering Peter's answer to the same question, breathed in Edwina's gardenia scent and wondered what would become of her.

Its sweet redolence still hung in the air. The curtains and shutters were closed for the day and the two women, seeing each other, shadowy, across the room, were on edge, facing the change from a known world to one where everything would be different.

Hassan returned. The taxis had been brought to the door and now the travellers could start on their journey. It was the congested hour of the morning and as the taxis were held up in traffic, Harriet became perturbed, imagining Guy losing patience at the station and perhaps going away. But they arrived in good time and he was nowhere to be seen. She put Marion into a carriage then ran from one end of the platform to the other, searching among groups of people, unable to find him. The guard, coming towards her, shutting the carriage doors and unfurling his green flag, called to the passengers to get on board.

The train was full of young mothers and children and Harriet, finding her carriage, was greeted with unusual buoyancy by Marion, happy at being in the company of others like herself.

Hanging from the window, feeling the train about to start, Harriet saw Guy making his way along the platform, searching short-sightedly for her face among the faces at the windows. She shouted to him and he came running, his glasses sliding down his nose, already beginning a lengthy excuse for failing to be there sooner. Someone had come into the office just as he was about to leave.

'Had to have a word with him ... Didn't realise ... So sorry ...'

The little time left to them was taken up by these excuses, yet what else was there to be said? Harriet stretched her hand down to him and he was able to hold it for a second or two before the train moved and drew it from his grasp. He followed the carriage at a jog-trot, still trying to tell her something but, whatever it was, it was lost in noise as the train gathered speed.

Leaning out further, waving to him, she could see him pushing his glasses up to his brow and straining to see her, but almost at once she was too far away to see or be seen.

Marion had kept a seat for her and she sank into it, unaware of the people about her, still holding to a vision of Guy standing, peering after the train, looking perplexed because he had lost sight of her. She did not suppose he would be perplexed for long. She could imagine, as he turned back to his own employments, his buttocks and shoulders moving with the energetic excitement of having so much to do.

And what would come of all that activity. He ate himself up. He dissipated himself in ephemeral entertainments like this show that would be a one-day's wonder and just about pay its way. To someone moving so rapidly through life, reality and unreality merged and were one and the same thing. There were times when she felt he drained her life as well as his own, but he had physical strength. He could renew himself and she could not.

He had said the climate was killing her but now, seeing the relationship from a distance, she felt the killing element was not the heat of Cairo but Guy himself.

Marion was sitting next to a woman Harriet did not know, but knew about. She was the Mrs Rutter who had once reproached Jake Jackman for being a civilian. A rich widow, she had about her the confident certainty of one who knew that her world was the only world that mattered. The war had not changed it much. She lived in one of the great houses on Gezira and kept a retinue of servants. Harriet wondered why she was leaving this land of plenty for their beleaguered homeland where she would be no more privileged than any other woman.

She was asking Marion probing little questions, keeping herself at a distance until she discovered that Marion's husband was a diplomat in Baghdad. At this, Mrs Rutter became affable and looked approvingly at Marion and made advances to Richard who was persuaded to give her a smile. She had on her knee a large shagreen jewel-case and Marion, returning favours, said, 'What a beautiful case!'

'Yes, it is beautiful,' Mrs Rutter warmly agreed: 'I *treasure* it. Whenever I travel, I carry it myself, heavy though it is.'

As they talked about the jewel case, Marion, holding Richard on her knee, put her cheek down on the top of his head, knowing she had the greater treasure.

They were now out in the desert and Mrs Rutter, saying the light was too keen for her, pulled down the dusty, dark blue oil-cloth blind over the carriage window. The window was open and the blind flapped in the wind. Richard closed his eyes, thinking night had fallen, and lay like a little ghost in Marion's arms.

The other passengers fell silent in the steamy penumbra and Mrs Rutter, not wishing to be overheard, whispered to Marion, apparently conveying facts too sacred to be widely circulated. In England, she said, she had a married daughter the same age as Marion. '*And* three little grandchildren. I've never seen them, so I'm going home to enjoy them while they're still babies.'

Enthralled by this information, Marion talked about her coming confinement: 'I'm sure Richard will be easier to deal with when he's not the only one. I always think one should have two or three.'

Mrs Rutter fervently agreed: 'What is a home without children?' she asked.

Harriet, not included in the conversation, thought '. . . or without a husband?' She could see between Marion and Mrs Rutter a swift growing up of friendship that was likely to intensify until, on board the ship, Marion would be a surrogate daughter to the old lady, Mrs Rutter a surrogate mother to the pregnant woman. As she felt the burden of Marion slip away from her, Harriet could see even less reason now for being on a train where the younger children were peevish, the older obstreperous and the grown-ups suffocating in semi-darkness.

Hours had passed, or so it seemed, when, pulling aside the blind, she saw the canal: a flat ribbon of turquoise water lying between dazzling flats of sand. They were coming into Suez. Between the grimy house-backs, hung with washing, she could see the bazaars and wished she could visit them. But the passengers were not here on a sight-seeing tour. The train ran straight on to the quay and they had their first sight of the ship. It had a name at last. It was called the *Queen of Sparta*.

For some reason, the classical allusion jolted Harriet with fear: an elusive fear. She could make nothing of it as they climbed down to the quay and stood in the sea wind with the sea, itself, lapping the quayside. Then another departure came to her mind, the departure from Greece. The refugees had embarked at the Piraeus among the burnt-out buildings, the water black with wrecks and wreckage. Only two ships rode upright: the *Erebus* and *Nox*.

They had been used to transport Italian prisoners-of-war to Egypt. They were vermin-ridden, filthy, red with rust, the life-boats useless because the davits had rusted. They were near derelict but the refugees had no choice. The situation compelled and they were thankful to have ships of any kind. They had to trust themselves to the *Erebus* and *Nox*; and the two old tankers had carried them gallantly across the sea to Alexandria.

The *Queen of Sparta*, painted umber, was the same colour as the tankers, but she looked trim enough. She was altogether a more seaworthy craft than the *Erebus* and *Nox*, yet Harriet, who had trusted the tankers, was afraid of her. While the other women busied themselves collecting children together, ordering their baggage and getting into line to embark, Harriet stood apart from them, feeling that no power on earth could get her on to the *Queen of Sparta*. But this, she knew, was ridiculous. She had had forebodings before without any resultant disasters and she must swallow back this foreboding and go with the others.

The queue stretched down the quay to the ship's gangway. Seeing Marion and Mrs Rutter about mid-way, she went reluctantly to join them, thinking, 'I want an excuse to escape. I want a last-minute reprieve.' And what hope of that?

Harriet's companions, still fused in the comfortable stimulation of their new relationship, scarcely saw that Harriet was with them. A truck was collecting the baggage. It had almost reached Harriet's place in the queue when she heard her name called.

Mortimer and her co-driver were walking towards her. Breaking from the queue, Harriet ran towards them, her arms outstretched, shouting, 'Mortimer! Mortimer! God has sent you to save me.'

Mortimer laughed: 'Save you from what?'

'I don't know. All I want is to get away from here. Take me with you.'

Harriet, seeing her luggage about to be thrown on to the truck, ran to retrieve it. She told Marion: 'I'm not going with you. You'll be all right, won't you? Mrs Rutter will look after you. I hope you and Richard have a pleasant journey.'

Baffled by Harriet's decision, Marion asked: 'You mean, you're going back to Cairo?'

'No, I'm going to Damascus.'

'Damascus!' Marion, parting her lips in disapproval, looked like a good little girl confronted by some piece of peccant naughtiness. She breathed out a shocked, 'Oh dear!' then, seeing the queue had moved forward, she hurried on as though fearing Mrs Rutter, too, might forsake her.

Mortimer came over to Harriet: 'We're driving through the night. I expect you can get some sleep among the ammunition in the back. Hope you won't mind a bumpy ride across Sinai? The road's in a bad way.'

Harriet laughed and said she did not mind how she crossed Sinai for all the wonders of the Levant were on the other side.

CODA

A week after the ship sailed, rumours reached Cairo that the *Queen of Sparta* had been torpedoed off Tanganyika with the loss of all on board. Then another, more detailed, report reached the *Egyptian Mail* from a correspondent in Dar-es-Salaam. One life-boat, crowded with women and children, had got away from the sinking ship. The steering was faulty. The boat was drifting when the German U-boat surfaced and the commander took on board a heavily pregnant woman and her small son. They were put to rest on the commander's own bunk but, a British cruiser appearing on the horizon, the U-boat had to submerge and the woman and child were returned to the life-boat. The cruiser did not sight the boat that drifted for ten days until found by fishermen who towed it into Delagoa Bay. By that time most of the children and many of the adults had died of thirst and exposure. No names were given.

That was the last that Cairo heard of the *Queen of Sparta* and, the times being what they were, only the bereaved gave further thought to the lost ship.